The rushing waters drowned out the din of the townspeople,

giving Meredith and Thatcher the illusion that they were in their own private world.

"And you are very good at what you do," she replied.

"Logging?"

"No. Being mysterious and aloof. In fact, I would call you an expert."

"From a reporter, I guess that's a compliment."

"Being elusive is not always a good idea." She gave him a saucy look. "Good day, Mr. Talbot."

Thatcher watched Meredith's not-so-elegant departure with amusement. Her boot caught in a hole, she wobbled, straightened herself again, gave her hat a fierce tug. . . . He chuckled. If he didn't know better, he'd say she'd flirted with him just now. What had she said? *Being elusive is not always a good idea. Now that could be taken several ways.*

DIANNE CHRISTNER resides in Arizona with her husband, Jim. Her son Mike lives in Arizona and her daughter Rachel attends college in Texas. Dianne, always a romantic at heart, delights in the happy-ever-afters. Six years ago, she left her clerical career to write fictional romance and incorporate the truths of God's love and happy-ever-after plans for His children. This is her fourth title for Heartsong. Other hobbies include bird watching, historical research, biblical study, reading, and antiquing, and most of all, spending time with family.

Books by Dianne Christner

HEARTSONG PRESENTS
HP80—Proper Intention
HP108—Lofty Ambitions
HP203—Ample Portions

Storm

Dianne Christner

Heartsong Presents

To my husband, Jim, whom I adore. Thanks for sticking with me through life's storms. Each day with you brings wonderful new discoveries. In awe, let us meet each tomorrow hand in hand, hearts locked together, sharing our love for each other and for our Lord.

To my Lord, thank You for bringing good out of the storms, for Your steadfast presence, Your grace and love.

To my sister, Chris, thanks for your encouragement and helping me with details of your beautiful redwood country.

A note from the author:
I love to hear from my readers! You may correspond with me by writing:
Dianne Christner
Author Relations
PO Box 719
Uhrichsville, OH 44683

ISBN 1-57748-757-5

STORM

Cover illustration by Kevin McClain.

PRINTED IN THE U.S.A.

prologue

The storm that blew through the offices of *McClure's* magazine was five-foot-four and brunette. Meredith S. Mears's middle initial stood for Storm. Whether her parents named Storm after her personality or whether her personality took shape around her name, the other reporters knew not, but one thing stood certain, the name accurately described her as she strode past.

Several pairs of male eyes followed the green skirt that swayed around tiny black-heeled lace-up boots. She marched to a door with a nameplate that read Asa Smythe, Editor, and her small hand shot up and knocked. They watched her hesitate, then turn the knob. The door opened and closed. One reporter cocked an eyebrow, another frowned, and the men returned to their work.

Meredith straightened to her full height and cleared her throat.

The comb-slicked top of a gray head whipped back, a deep voice broke the silence of the room. "What can I do for you, Storm?"

She slapped down her latest article on his desk. "I want a real assignment."

The editor did not flinch, only nodded his head toward the chair that faced his desk. "Why don't you sit down, and let's discuss this matter like two civilized people."

Meredith seated herself, planted both feet firmly on the floor and clasped her hands in her lap to keep them from trembling. The man across the desk, with nerves like steel, was not only her editor, he was the one person who knew how

5

to help her keep her goals in perspective and meet them. To be a journalist—in a man's world in the year 1899—was not an easy thing. Asa Smythe made it easier.

"Now then, what determines a real assignment, Storm?"

"Covering a subject that makes a difference in the world, writing something other than the society column, fashion reviews, or advertisements."

"Did you ever stop to think that your position at *McClure's*, in and of itself, is doing just that for the advancement of women?"

"That's not my purpose here, and you know it."

"It may not be your purpose, but it is the issue."

"This is not about women. It is about me doing something worthwhile."

Asa straightened the paperwork on his desk. "And what are these pressing concerns that you harbor?"

She leaned forward. "You know how I hate it when people or animals get mistreated or hurt." The fine lines on Asa's face deepened. It was true, she could not stand seeing any living thing hurt.

"I've read some of John Muir's writings," she continued. "Last week I had the chance to hear him speak on the issue of conservation of the western forests. He portrays the tree as a living thing. His speech has been nagging at me all week. Something needs to be done before the loggers use up all the good timber out West, as they have in the East."

"Oh, no." Asa shook his head. "You cannot even think that I would send you on such an assignment."

"It is exactly what I'm thinking. It would be perfect for me." She stood and paced the room. "Think about this angle, a woman's view of the backwoods, the Wild West. It would be romantic."

"Romantic! What are you thinking?"

"It would make a great series! I could get inside the heads that fell the trees, the minds that make the money. From a female perspective, I could. . ."

"Stop right there. Do you have any idea what a loggers' camp is like?"

"Well, no. That's just it. Neither does the average person. I could make this story come alive. I know I could."

"It is impossible. Why, once a man becomes a logger, his life expectancy is only seven years."

She shook her head, and a dark strand worked loose from her upswept hairdo. Her slender fingers hastily tucked it back into place. "What has that got to do with anything?"

"It means, young lady, that your life expectancy in such a place would probably be about seven days."

"Exaggerating a wee bit, aren't we?"

"How would a woman with your good looks survive in such an uncivilized place? Where would you stay?"

Her chin rose. "I've done a bit of research myself. I'll choose a camp that's close to civilization, and I'll take along a male photographer."

Asa groaned something incoherent, then said, "No. It is out of the question. I am sure we can find something safer that would suit you."

Meredith placed both palms on the desk across from him, her face close to his. "I can do it. Please, Asa. It is something that I need to do, either for *McClure's* or on my own, but I'd rather do it for you."

"Go away. Let me think."

"Yes, sir." Before she reached the door, she turned back. "One more thing. I have in mind the California logging camps. I could take the Overland Limited all the way to San Francisco. It's only a three-day trip from Chicago, and going by rail is ever so safe these days."

"Storm."

"Yes?"

"Please, go away."

Another nod, and Meredith was out of the editor's office. She whisked past the other reporters with a smug smile, her thoughts already far away. *Hmm, what clothes will I need in*

San Francisco? Before Meredith packed any clothes, however, she had an unpleasant chore to attend to, another call to make.

❧

She knocked at the door of the house where she was raised. The door creaked open, and her father's hazel eyes rested on her, then closed like iron gates. The lines around his eyes and mouth sagged. He shrugged stiff shoulders and left her standing on the stoop. Because she was expected to follow him, she did. The way he hunkered down at the paperwork strewn on the kitchen table, it was obvious he didn't want to be bothered. But Meredith tried. She placed the latest edition of the *McClure's* on the table beside him. He merely glanced at the printed intrusion and left it lay.

A pot of coffee warmed on the stove, so she poured them each a cup. "I have an assignment." Instead of giving her a reply, her father took a swig of his drink. "I'm going to California to do a story on forest conservation."

He eyed her over the rim of his cup, and Storm took a gulp of the bitter liquid while she waited. Her father picked up the *McClure's* issue and squashed a fly with it, then tossed the magazine on the floor by his feet. "If you go west, then you're a bigger fool than I thought."

Meredith slammed the cup down with a rattle; coffee splattered her father's paperwork.

"I need to get far away from you. You never have loved me." With tears welling up, she strode past him and slammed the door on her way out.

Inside the house, her father's arm lashed out and swept across the table. Papers scattered and floated down to the floor over shattered glass. His head dropped into his hands, and he combed his fingers through his hair, wondering how his life had gotten to such a low point. *She's right.* He leaned his old bones over the side of his chair and groped for the magazine that mattered so much to Meredith.

one

The train screeched, iron scraping against iron, and lurched forward to start Meredith on her westward journey. Without a bit of regret, she watched the depot disappear from view. After coughing up cinders, the locomotive clacked up momentum, eventually settling into a comfortable rhythm of motion. Beside her, Jonah Shaw thumbed open a red and white cloth-covered book entitled *An Adventure in Photography*.

"Have you been west before?" she asked her traveling escort.

"Mm-hmm. Once."

The fifty-year-old photographer had an attitude that reminded Meredith of a crusty old schoolmaster she'd once had, who rapped his students across the knuckles with a stick when they became too rambunctious.

She hunched close. "Did you like it?"

He slowly lowered his book to his lap. "I never decided."

"I think I shall like it."

"Why?"

"I hear it's a vast land with plenty of room to prove some things."

He did not reply, but raised his book until the only part of his face visible was his smooth bald forehead.

She patted his arm. "Don't be so stuffy, Jonah." He flinched, and when she saw that she would not get any more out of him, she set her mind to work. Within moments, she had come up with a way to pass the time. She reached down by her feet for her brown leather portfolio. It was full of writing materials, and while most women carried parasols, this portfolio accompanied Meredith wherever she went.

"Excuse me, please."

"Where are you going?" Small, stern eyes peered over his book.

"I've come up with an idea for a great story. Asa will love it."

"But where are you going?"

She stepped over him. "To interview the passengers." Meredith kept her back to Jonah, sensing his wary eyes upon her. *He'll soon get tired of doing that.* She worked her way to a vacant seat and fine prospect. "May I join you a moment?"

A woman with a tiny baby in her arms and another child playing at her ankles considered her peculiar request.

"Of course. It's my son's seat, but he's inclined to play right now."

Meredith looked at the fuzzy-haired boy whose pudgy hands were exploring the fabric seams of the train's seat.

"He seems an intelligent, inquisitive lad to say the least. My name is Meredith S. Mears. I'm a reporter. I'm doing a story on the people who take the Overland Limited. Would you mind telling me about your travels?"

"Going to Chicago to visit some relatives."

"Traveling alone with children. What a brave soul you are."

"Thank you."

Meredith caressed the baby's dimpled cheek. "Have a good trip."

Next she worked her way toward an interesting subject, a square-faced woman who wore a diamond brooch and traveled with a servant. There were no empty seats, so Meredith merely hovered over the woman as she introduced herself and her intentions.

"I think not." The woman placed her hand over her ample bosom and turned her angular face toward the passing landscape.

Meredith straightened her torso. A reporter never gives up, so she cast a quick look about the train to see whom she should interview next. But the tracks made a sharp curve, and the sudden sway of the train sent her reeling across the aisle in utter helplessness.

Some hands reached out to steady her. She bumped her

elbow hard on one of the seats. Her paper flew up and her pen rolled away, down the aisle. It took several helpful gentlemen to get everything straightened out. With a gush of apologies, she stumbled back down the aisle, across Jonah's legs, and collapsed into her seat. She did not look at him as she rubbed her throbbing elbow.

"Have you proven anything yet?" Jonah asked from behind his book.

Meredith did not reply. Before long, the pain in her arm subsided, and she eased back into the corner of her seat and closed her eyes.

ᐓ

Meredith awoke to the sound of the train's shrill whistle and the conductor's call, "Chicago Station."

It took about an hour to detrain, check on their luggage, find something to eat, and board their next train. This one would take them to their destination. It was long and full of Pullman sleeping cars, dining cars, smoking cars, plush seats, and every convenience known to travelers.

"Perhaps you'd like the aisle this time?" Jonah asked.

"Yes, please." Meredith set down her portfolio and straightened the pins in her hair.

At last the train wheels turned; the floor rumbled at Meredith's feet. City buildings passed in and out of view, making Meredith dizzy until they had picked up speed and entered the greener countryside. When the slight discomfort of head and stomach subsided, Meredith reverted to scrutinizing the other passengers, still intent on continuing her interviews.

One man, in particular, who occupied a window seat just across the aisle, caught her interest. His melancholy gaze was fixed on the passing scenery. Meredith sensed a hurt or regret of some sort in those soft brown eyes and wondered about his life. It only seemed natural to ease into the seat next to him.

"Hello."

ᐓ

Thatcher Talbot jerked his gaze from the window and stared

in disbelief at the forward woman, her autumn-colored eyes sympathetic yet gently probing. There was a dusting of ginger across her nose and cheeks. A multitude of thoughts rushed through his mind. *I noticed her when she boarded the train.* He remembered feeling a bit envious of the balding man that accompanied her.

"I'm Meredith S. Mears, New York reporter. Doing a story on the people who travel the Overland Limited."

He stared at her extended hand, and the urge to press it to his lips left him with a voice of warning. *Reporter. She'll expose you.*

After a considerable pause, the woman dropped her hand. Her voice took on a professional tone. "May I ask you a few questions?"

See! The warning voice gloated. He frowned. "No, I was about to get some much-needed rest." Then he stretched his legs, cocked his hat to block out the world with its nosey reporters, and slouched in his seat.

From beneath his hidey-hole, his face burned when he heard the passenger one seat behind him offer, "You can interview me."

❧

Meredith felt a prick of hurt and turned from the uncooperative passenger to the voice beckoning her. Once Meredith accumulated enough material for her story, she started back toward her seat, careful to watch for the quirks of the train. A keen desire to steal another glance across the aisle at the man with the melancholy expression could not be suppressed.

He was gone.

❧

Three days later, a wilted and wrinkled Meredith stepped down from the train that had whisked her across a continent. She raised her arm to shade her eyes from the sun, gave a small cough to expel the dust from her lungs, and gazed at the new world that received her, San Francisco.

"I'll go get our baggage and be right back," Jonah said. He

removed his hat to wipe his brow, then replaced it on his smooth head.

"Thank you." Meredith pointed with a gloved hand. "I'll wait over there, out of the way."

"Good."

Meredith had learned from experience that one of the best ways to encounter a new situation was to stand back and study how things were done. A welcome summer breeze ruffled her skirt, and she reached up to straighten her hat with one hand while the other clutched her brown leather portfolio.

Tall buildings on streets that ran straight toward the sky surrounded the depot. The tang of sea air and the aroma of food from nearby vendors mixed with the sooty foul smells from the trains. Soon her attention settled onto some familiar faces from the trip. "Good luck to you," she called out to a fellow passenger, giving him a wave.

The woman with the large diamond brooch strutted by with a small group of people. Meredith caught the words "new woman." The accusation hurt. That was the name going around for the progressive women who were stepping out of social boundaries with the turn of the new century. Meredith, however, did not consider herself a part of that radical group. She had nothing to prove to the world about being a woman. She only needed to prove to her father. . .well, she certainly would not think about that today.

A trickle of sweat ran down her brow, and an unfeminine wetness beneath her arms caused discomfort. She noticed a line of horse-drawn hackneys and wondered if she should secure one, when Jonah's thin but sturdy figure appeared with a porter. She fell into step with them as they made their way to a hackney. The driver stood by his rig.

"We need a hotel close to a cable car and a post office, and we'll be needing to get some supplies. We're heading north into the wilderness," Meredith said.

The driver glanced at Jonah, saw his nod, then replied, "I know just the place, ma'am."

Meredith smiled and stepped up into the hackney with Jonah close behind her.

"Was your equipment all right?"

Her traveling partner smiled. "All intact."

"My typewriter?"

"Fine."

"Good." When the coach took off, her head snapped back, and she reached up to secure her hat.

❧

The Old Mission Hotel, a low adobe structure with a wide veranda across the front, hugged a small hill and provided a contrast to the more common Victorian inns they had passed. Two rooms were secured. After they inspected their rooms and tucked away their belongings, Meredith met Jonah in the hotel lobby to discuss their plans.

"I thought we might find the closest land office and do some inquiring," she said.

He raised an eyebrow. "You mean you haven't chosen a camp yet?"

Her eyes lit. "That, Jonah, is our objective."

"But Asa said that you—"

"What Asa doesn't know won't hurt him, will it?" She patted his hand. "Don't worry so. We'll see what's available and decide tonight over supper."

Jonah stood. "Perhaps I was too hasty to jump on this assignment. . . ." His voice trailed off, but Meredith didn't wait around to hear his next complaint.

❧

The land office wasn't far. When their business was concluded, she took Jonah's arm and chatted all the way back to the hotel. Inside the lobby, she patted her portfolio.

"I'm going to my room to look over this information. Shall we meet at dinner to discuss our plans?"

"I suppose so," Jonah said.

"Look, Jonah. This assignment is not a contest between us. We need to work as a team. Sometimes it feels as if you have a problem with me."

"A man likes to take the lead once in a while."

"Whenever you feel the urge to do so, go right ahead."

He stroked the downward tips of his mustache. "We'll see, Storm."

Still, she hesitated to leave. "There's one other thing."

"What's that?"

"Once we get to the logging camp, I'd rather you didn't call me that name in front of other people."

"It's your name."

"I know, but I have a feeling this isn't going to be an easy assignment, and I don't want to give a wrong impression to any of those loggers. Know what I mean?"

"Yeah. I guess I do."

&

At dinner, they agreed that Bucker's Stand would be the most convenient logging camp to investigate. Its location was north of San Francisco in the redwood country. The closest town, called Buckman's Pride, was situated on the coast.

"The way I look at it," Meredith said, "we have two choices. Either we can go by ship, or we can find us an overland guide."

"Any ideas where we would find such a person?" Jonah asked.

"I've been thinking about that. Most loggers coming from the East pass through San Francisco. I'd wager that some of them pick up supplies while they're in the big city. We just have to figure out where they purchase them."

Jonah's blue eyes sparkled. "That just might work." He leaned close across the table. "If we could find such a place, we could hold off making our decision until we talked to a few of them, get their advice on the best method of travel."

"Good idea." Meredith beamed, then stifled a yawn. "Well, now that we have that settled, I think I'll go to my room. I need to finish up my Overland Limited story so we can get it posted tomorrow."

"Go ahead. I'll just mingle down here a bit and see if I can glean any information about where your loggers buy their supplies."

"Good idea." She patted his hand. "Good night, then."

"Good night, Storm."

❧

The next morning Jonah greeted Meredith with news that he knew where the loggers purchased their supplies.

"Wonderful! Is the postal office on the way?"

"I believe so. We'll need to take the cable car."

They ate breakfast at the hotel, walked to the post office to mail Meredith's story, then rode the cable car to a shop called the Outfitters. With Meredith's first step inside, the heel of her shoe caught in a gaping hole.

Jonah's hand shot out to steady her. "Watch your step." He nodded at a nearby man. She followed Jonah's gaze to the man's boots. They had spikes in them. "Loggers' boots," he whispered. "That's what's tearing up the floor. I guess we're in the right place."

Meredith smelled the masculine scents of leather and tobacco. Her eyes roamed over the displays of tools, leather goods, clothing, bedrolls, rolls of canvas, coils of rope, liniments, and books. Along the wall lined with tools such as picks, shovels, axes, and handsaws, she caught a snatch of conversation between two men. She heard them mention Bucker's Stand, and that was all she needed.

She walked up behind them. "Excuse me, sir." The men did not turn around to acknowledge her. She glanced at Jonah. He hesitated, then cleared his throat. The men quit talking.

"Pardon me, may I have a word with you, sir?" Meredith asked.

The closest man turned to face her, while the other tipped his hat at Jonah and went back to his shopping. The well-cut tan suede vest enhanced the man's masculine form. She looked up expectantly, and to her ill fate, into familiar brown eyes. The melancholy man from the train. She hadn't realized he was so handsome.

He smiled and stared at her for an uncomfortably long period of time before asking, "Did you want something?"

Her face heated. "Yes. In passing, I overheard you mention Bucker's Stand. May I ask, are you headed there?"

The man removed his hat and smirked. "I am."

"The reason I ask is, my friend and I are looking for someone to guide us, accompany us, to Buckman's Pride."

"I'm sorry, I can't be of help." He replaced his hat and turned to go.

"Wait." She grabbed his sleeve. "We can pay." He stopped, looked at her, then at his arm. Instantly, she released him. "I. . . I'm sorry."

"So am I." Then he was gone.

Jonah had observed the entire scene. "I thought we were going to find out what the overland trip was like before we offered to pay someone to guide us."

She leaned against a shelf filled with boxes of nails. "We were. I don't know what's gotten into me. I've never acted so unprofessionally. It's that. . .that man. When I saw him, I couldn't think clearly. Why, he makes my blood boil!"

Jonah lifted a wooly eyebrow that matched his brown mustache in color. "Well, I hope we don't meet up with him again. He seems to bring out some mighty strange behavior in you. If I didn't know better, I'd think you were smitten with him."

"What!" She jerked away from the wall, and her hand struck a shovel that clattered to the floor. "That is utterly ridiculous. You know me better than that." A clerk appeared to pick up the shovel and straighten tools. She stepped away, then had to jerk her foot loose from where it had sunk deep into a groove in the wooden plank. "Let's just get back to work, shall we?"

≈

By midafternoon, Meredith and Jonah had nearly concluded their business. They would travel by land, and they had secured a guide. They stayed in the Outfitters long enough to make several purchases. Meredith did not miss how Jonah's eyes widened when she examined the men's clothing, cut in a very small size.

"Get yourself some loggers' clothing, Jonah. We'll fit in better when we reach the camp."

"I don't see anything here that appeals to my sense of. . ."

"Nonsense!" she interrupted, grabbing his sleeve. "Here." She placed a set of trousers in his arms. "And you'll probably need this." Another article slapped him across the shoulder.

"If you insist that I wear these duds, then move out of the way, Storm. I'll do my own choosing."

"You don't need to get in a huff about it. I'll work on the rest of our list. It was so good of our guide to make it for us."

Jonah pointed. "Better get some different shoes while you're at it."

"You're absolutely correct," she said, and noticed the glitter of surprise in his eyes.

After that, they each purchased a set of saddlebags, and Jonah bargained with the store owner to trade their travelling trunks for several leather bags. When all the arrangements for their trip were in order, Meredith and Jonah returned to their hotel to dine and retire early. They would leave in the morning.

two

Meredith rose early and dressed in her newly purchased male attire. She hesitated outside the hotel lobby. The clothes she could get used to, but not the abominable hat.

She owned a multitude, all colorful and elaborately embellished with feathers and bows and birds and whatever attracted her attention and her delight. But this one was plain brown and round like a soup bowl with a large brim, which she supposed was to shield her face from the sun. It also hid her long brown hair, secured beneath in a tidy knot. Her hand crept up to examine. . .

"Storm! You're up."

Meredith jerked her hand down. "Don't do that!"

"Sorry," Jonah said with a grin. "I didn't mean to frighten you." He studied her. "Sensible clothes. Let's have breakfast."

She felt relieved that her travelling companion awoke on the congenial side, yet she regretted his catching her in a vain moment.

❧

Breakfast was hot and filling. Soon they were outside the hotel. Their guide, Silas Cooke, appeared right on time.

Meredith strode toward him. "Good morning, Mr. Cooke."

Silas Cooke watched her with skepticism; his eyes flitted across Jonah, then returned to her with a new brightness. "Good morning to you, Miss Mears." His blue gaze ran over her appraisingly, and his beard gave an odd twitch. "Didn't recognize you right off. See you're a sensible woman."

Jonah chuckled. "I've heard her called a 'new woman' repeatedly, but never 'sensible.' "

Meredith gave Jonah a cutting look. "You said so just this morning."

Jonah stared at her feet. "I said your clothes were sensible. By the way, those boots look comfortable."

"We're wasting time," Meredith said.

Silas brought around the horses and two pack mules. Meredith needed assistance mounting the smallest horse. She imagined her riding would improve on this assignment. For some reason this small challenge gave her great satisfaction, and poised straight in the saddle, she felt eager to start the assignment of a lifetime.

Meredith soon shed her self-consciousness where her clothing was concerned. No one gave her a second look. Loggers and miners passing through San Francisco were a commonplace event. The morning passed pleasantly without incident. Jonah pointed out the tall Call Building, which housed the San Francisco newspaper.

They boarded a ferry once, where Meredith marveled over the flocks of pelicans and caught a wonderful view of the Cliff House, a mansion turned into a famous eating establishment. After that, they mounted up again and turned their back to the hills and harbors of San Francisco with all its bustling civilization.

The trail meandered along the coastline, providing a fearsome sight. The edge of the earth broke off hundreds of feet above rock and water. At times the narrow path hugged so close to the cliffs that Meredith's heart would pound with fright, and she would force herself to think of something other than toppling over the bluff and into the slapping white foam so far below.

Her legs and shoulders ached, not only from the long hours of riding but from tensing her muscles in fear. Meredith welcomed every opportunity to dismount and stretch her miserable legs. *I might learn to ride better, if I live that long.*

That night at camp, Meredith went for a short walk along the cliffs. A ship bobbed at sea, birds shrieked overhead, and the feel of the moist, salty air was cold against her face.

"Water as far as the eye can see."

She jerked her head around. Silas gazed out over the scenic panorama. "It's incredible. Makes me feel like a tiny dot in the universe," she said.

"Take a good look. Tomorrow, we're going to move inland."

Their camp nestled securely within the shelter of some large rocks. Silas unloaded some supplies from one of the pack mules. He cooked their supper over an open fire. Meredith inhaled the food, then felt her eyes droop.

Silas nudged her. "Smooth out a spot, like this, for your bedroll."

She followed his instructions, and before she knew what had happened, the light of day shone again, and it was time to climb back up into the saddle.

The trail turned rugged and hilly and wound through dense forest with trees huge and plentiful enough to stretch the imagination of any easterner, and Meredith wondered if conservation was even an issue here, in the West. That evening she felt sore and stiff, but able to do her part in setting up camp.

After their meal of smoked ham, beans, and biscuits, Silas pulled out a chunk of wood he carried with him and started to whittle. "I worried about this part of the trip. But you're an excellent outdoorsman," Meredith said.

"I agree. I don't know how you do it, but you make us quite comfortable with our scanty provisions," Jonah said.

"Just natural. I've lived my life in the wilds." Silas laid the wood on his thigh, reached into his trousers for a pint of whiskey, and took a swig.

"How long have you been in logging?" Meredith asked.

"Most my life. I only regret I missed the gold rush. Course it didn't make my grandpap rich."

The gold brought him, but he fell in love with the land."

"Mm," Meredith said.

"It does grow on you," Jonah said.

"Wait until tomorrow."

Meredith wondered if Silas would even be able to ride the

next day, with all the whiskey he consumed. She fell asleep to tales about Silas's grandpap's gold-digging days.

But Silas rose sharp as the sole on a logger's boot. Meredith need not have worried. About midday, she found out what Silas meant the night before when he said, "Wait until tomorrow."

❧

First, she heard it, a roaring sound coming from the hills, which grew louder as they rode farther up the trail. Silas stopped his mount, and then she saw the most beautiful waterfalls in the world.

They ate at the majestic spot. Jonah unloaded enough equipment to take photographs while Silas watered the horses. Meredith found a secluded place to sponge bathe. Afterwards, they followed the river west until they came to a shallow place, calm enough to ford.

On the far side, Meredith twisted in her saddle for a final look. "Must we leave it behind?"

"I reckon you want us to build you a castle here," Silas said.

"No, I expect not. I enjoy civilization too much. But it is something to remember."

They rode harder after that to reach the location where Silas wanted to camp that night.

❧

The next day a different sight tugged Meredith's heartstrings, acres and acres of destroyed forests. The damage gouged deep into the woods and stretched a couple miles along the trail.

"What caused this, Silas? Fire?"

"It's just stripped from logging."

"But it's horrible."

"There's plenty more trees, ma'am. Don't worry about it none." She cast Jonah a look of concern. "We'll have to take some pictures, Silas."

It was time for the West to think about conservation.

three

After several long days of travel, nights camping under the stars, innumerable saddle blisters, and unmentionable aches and pains, Meredith's horse trotted back into civilization. It was not New York, Chicago, or San Francisco, but a form of civilization. Meredith tipped her head back to peer out from under the abominable hat.

There was a hotel, a saloon, and several stores farther uphill, yapping dogs, barefoot children, but mostly there were men. She strained her eyes to catch a glimpse of skirt, or lace, or a pretty hat or two. A large sawmill prevailed over all of the other establishments, usurping more than its share of property, people, and town noise. It would be a good place to begin her investigation of the lumber world. The town was perfect, better than she had expected.

Silas delivered them to the front stoop of the only hotel in Buckman's Pride and bade them farewell. Meredith assured him they would meet again, and something in the twinkling of his eyes gave Meredith to believe that the lumberjacks would probably hear of her presence long before she stepped foot into their camp.

The elderly hotel clerk was courteous and kind enough to head them in the direction of permanent lodging. They had two options, get a discount price at the hotel or inquire with a Mrs. Amelia Cooper who oftentimes took in boarders. Meredith and Jonah made plans to bathe, change into proper clothing, and immediately search out the woman.

❧

"My name is Meredith S. Mears, and this is my business associate, Jonah Shaw. We heard you might take us as boarders."

"Glad to meet you. I'm Mrs. Cooper. You two married?"

"No, ma'am," Jonah said, hat in his hand.

"I don't allow any unlawful male-female goings-on. . . ."

"Oh no." Meredith shook her head. "I am a reporter from New York City, and Jonah is a photographer. We've come to do a story for *McClure's* magazine. We would need two rooms, and I can assure you that all that will be taking place between us is strictly," she paused to smile, "journalism at its best."

The woman, tall, large-boned, with a plain but pleasant face, studied them, hat to boot. Meredith made her own observations. The woman dressed and handled herself with social grace. Meredith could read Mrs. Cooper's mind. *One of those eastern reporters.*

"What kind of story are you doing?"

"One on Bucker's Stand logging camp."

"Nothing harmful, I hope."

Meredith flashed the woman a smile. "I hope not, too."

"I see." Mrs. Cooper took several moments to digest this. "I do have two rooms that I could let to you. Would you like to see them now?"

"Oh please," Meredith said. She cast Jonah a hopeful smile, and they followed the landlady's swishing yellow gown, which was to Meredith an unexpected article in such a back-woodsy place. Mrs. Cooper paused for them to look into a formal but cozy parlor. It consisted of mahogany furniture with comfortable-looking quilted backs, a rosewood shelf clock, Victorian lamps with tassels and butterflies, a well-worn floral rug, and a fireplace.

Must be a wealthy widow stuck here for some reason.

They passed down a short hall and up a flight of stairs. At the far end of the upstairs hall, two vacant rooms were located across from each other.

"I only have these two rooms available, no other boarders right now."

The first was small but furnished with a desk. "Perfect," Meredith said.

"Would you have a small room where I could develop photographs?" Jonah asked.

"Hmm." Mrs. Cooper rubbed her chin. "Let me think a moment."

Meanwhile, Jonah inspected the other room.

"There's the shed out back." Mrs. Cooper pointed toward the window. "Since my husband died, I only use it for storage. Things would have to be rearranged."

"I'd have to hang my photographs."

"Yes," she nodded. "I think we could work out something."

"Good," Jonah said. "When can we move in?"

"Tomorrow."

Reporter and photographer waltzed back toward the hotel, exuberant over their good fortune.

"The lodgings couldn't be more perfect," Meredith said.

"I agree. This is going to be a pleasant assignment. Buckman's Pride," Jonah said with satisfaction, "a civilized place."

Even though Meredith was just as pleased with their new accommodations and also excited about the assignment, she said, "I'll hold my judgment for a later time, on the West, be it wild or tame. But I do believe. . . Look! Look there. A dress shop. And there are hats in the window."

Jonah peered through the glass at the display. "What do you think of the West now?"

"Well, the styles are certainly not the latest thing," she said, "but they're fine enough." She pointed. "Look at that yellow number with the green ostrich feather. It is most delightful."

"It would go nicely with your brown riding skirt, better yet your men's trousers."

"Scoundrel."

He took her elbow. "Come along, Storm. We didn't come here to shop."

As they started off, someone caught Meredith's attention. She didn't mean to stare, but the back of the man's head looked familiar. His shirtsleeves were rolled up, and large arms bulged as they heaved supplies into the back of a wagon.

Then he turned, and his face came into view. It was that man again! She swallowed and tightened her grip upon Jonah's arm. What was wrong with her? Just because he was the most handsome man she'd ever seen was no reason to ogle. She tore her eyes away and straightened her stance. He had been rude to her on the train and at the Outfitters. He was nothing to her. She would think about something else.

"Jonah. As soon as we're settled in, I want to visit the sawmill."

"That mill will provide some great photographs. I can't wait to get started."

They discussed plans for their assignment, and Meredith puffed under the steep incline of the street. "Not so fast, Jonah. This climb is taxing."

"Forgive me, Storm." He slowed his pace.

A team of horses clattered past, pulling a wagon. "Eek!" Mud splattered Meredith from hat to boot. "Of all the. . ." She wiped her face with her sleeve and peered, unbelieving, at the back of the driver of the wagon that had just plastered them with grime. "It's him!" she spat.

"Who?" Jonah asked. He, too, brushed off specks of mud, though Meredith had received the brunt of the avalanche. "Do you know him?"

"Of course! The man from Outfitters! That rude, horrible man!"

Jonah squinted at the wagon in disbelief just as it topped the hill. The man didn't even realize what he'd done.

Meredith's hands fluttered up. "And he's ruined my hat."

"Come along, missy. Let's get you back to the hotel."

She hiked up her skirt a few inches and stomped up the hill, now oblivious to the steep incline.

four

The hotel manager arranged for a hired wagon so Meredith and Jonah could move their belongings and equipment to Mrs. Cooper's. Once they arrived, she gave them keys to their rooms.

Meredith circled the pile of leather bags, which had been plunked down in the center of her room, wondering where to start. Mrs. Cooper gave a soft rap on her door.

"Come in."

The landlady smoothed back several gray-streaked blond hairs. "I hope everything is satisfactory. If there is anything else I can do to make your stay more comfortable, please let me know."

"Everything is perfect." Meredith's eyes ran across the small window above the desk. "It seems you've thought of everything and arranged the room just as I would have."

"After so many boarders, it gets a little easier. Dinner is at six. I only do breakfast and dinner." Meredith nodded. "I'll just check in on Mr. Shaw, now. I need to show him the shed he'll be using."

"Please, tell Jonah that I'll help him as soon as I'm finished here."

"I will." Mrs. Cooper nodded and the stray hairs worked free again.

Once the door had closed, Meredith unclasped the leather bags. Her clothing went into a wardrobe in hopes the wrinkles would not need to be steamed. Her hats she arranged and rearranged about the room, some on hooks by the door. *That looks cheery.* When her personal belongings were in place, she dove into the writing supplies and organized those on the desk by the window.

She retrieved her typewriter, handling it like a piece of fine china, and positioned it in its place of honor, center front of her desk. She traced the gold ornate lettering, *The Chicago,* across the front of its black cover and inspected all of the keys and parts.

Satisfied, she took a final inventory of the room. Her gaze lingered upon the mud-splattered green velvet and black-rimmed hat, and she crossed the room to it, plucked it off its peg, and dropped it into an empty bag. Next, she rearranged her desk. With a satisfactory nod, she pulled open the curtains above the desk. Jonah was in the backyard by the shed. *Perfect. I can see when he's in his studio.* With a song on her lips, she closed the curtains and changed into an old gown.

১৯

Just as she arrived at the shed's open door, a cloud of dust accosted her. With a cough, she jumped back.

"Is that you, Storm?"

Another cough. "Yes, it is."

Jonah's head peeked out, then the rest of him appeared, his hands gripping a broom handle. "Sorry about that. I didn't know anyone was about."

"So I see. Looks like you're doing serious housecleaning."

"Come, look," Jonah said. "This place is going to be great."

He stepped back inside, and Meredith tiptoed in behind him. Cobwebs scalloped the cluttered room. "I'm glad you're so excited. It looks like a lot of work to me."

"Oh, you're right there. Mrs. Cooper said that most of this stuff can go down to the mill. I'm going to move everything outside and let her tell me what goes and what stays. The rest she'll take inside the house."

"Why the mill?" Meredith asked.

"Didn't she tell you? Her late husband was a partner of Cooper's Mill. She figures the mill's owner can use some of this."

"Really. What can I do to help?"

"Hmm. Maybe you should sweep down cobwebs," Jonah

said, offering her the broom. "And I'll start dragging these crates outside."

"Done," Meredith said.

By the time they had emptied the old building of every tool, bucket, boot, and fishing pole, Mrs. Cooper poked her head inside. "You've been working so hard out here. I thought you might welcome a snack."

"Thank you, Mrs. Cooper. How thoughtful," Jonah said.

Mrs. Cooper pushed the tray of milk and cookies at him.

Meredith and Jonah perched on crates to enjoy the snack while Mrs. Cooper shuffled through boxes and rattled off instructions.

"This must be hard for you," Jonah said.

"It is. James was as good of a man as they come. But this needed to be done sometime, so don't worry about it."

Jonah nodded.

By early afternoon, the mopped-down shed was as clean as it would get. Meredith rubbed her palms on the skirt of her gown. "It looks real good, Jonah."

"Did you want to go to the mill with me?"

"Now?"

"After I locate that hired wagon. That'll give you time to change clothes and freshen up." He brushed a cobweb from her hair.

"Think I need it?"

Jonah gestured with a small wave. "I won't venture a reply to that. But if you wish, meet me here after I get things loaded, and we'll go to the mill together."

Meredith sneezed. "Oops. I'll be here."

&

Cooper's sawmill backed up against the Mad River a mile from where it spilled into the ocean. Buckman's Pride situated itself with its right arm resting along the river and its left arm embracing the ocean. The river produced the power to run the giant circular saws. They cut the large logs that came downriver from the logging camp. Because these redwood logs dwarfed any trees on the East Coast, the saws loomed bigger than any Jonah had ever seen.

"Look at those," Jonah pointed. "I've never seen anything so huge."

"I've never seen anything so fearful," Meredith said. "It all looks so dangerous."

The operation mesmerized them until a mill worker passed nearby, shouldering a bundle of leather straps. He shouted out, "Need some help?"

"Yes, sir," Jonah answered. "Have some business with the owner."

"You'll find him in there." The man nodded toward a nearby building, then continued on.

Jonah took Meredith's elbow and directed her toward the place the worker had indicated. Inside the warehouse, shingles were stacked in pallets along the wall. Beyond that was another door. They went to it, and Jonah knocked. Meredith straightened her hat.

"Come in," a deep voice drawled.

They entered. Two men occupied the room; one sat behind a desk and the other stood in the middle of the room.

Jonah strode to the desk. "I'm Jonah Shaw, New York photographer." The gray-haired man leaned over his desk and shook Jonah's offered hand. Meredith rushed forward. "Meredith S. Mears, journalist with *McClure's* magazine."

"Clement Washington," the owner said, also taking Meredith's hand. He settled back in his chair. "Seems to be my lucky day. You reporters know something I don't?" His question lumped them together like so much dead wood. "As if I don't have a business to run around here. Why don't you just talk to Ralston, here, so I don't need to repeat myself."

Deep furrows edged Frederick Ralston's frown. He introduced himself as a reporter for the Buckman's Pride newspaper.

"I don't mind people nosing about my business, exactly," Clement Washington said in his southern accent, "but I'm a busy man." He rose as if the matter was settled, and they were all dismissed. "Maybe some other time."

"Mrs. Cooper sent us," Jonah said. Clement jerked up his head and listened. "I've set up a studio in her shed, and in the process, we've cleaned out some of Mr. Cooper's belongings. She asked me to bring his things to you. They're crated up," he motioned, "outside in a wagon."

"Oh? Well, that's a different story." The mill's owner took a step toward Jonah and slapped his arm. "Let's go see what you've got."

They followed him outside, Jonah matching stride with the southerner.

Meredith lagged behind with the newspaperman. "I'm excited to learn that there is a newspaper in Buckman's Pride."

"Why is that?" The reporter's tone was frigid.

She shrugged her shoulders. "Just love the business."

"There isn't any room here for another reporter. It's a small operation."

"Is that so?"

Meredith pranced off and caught up with Clement Washington and Jonah. "I've never seen anything as excellent as these redwoods." Her breath came in heavy spurts. "How far do you ship your lumber? It must be in great demand."

"It is." Pride laced his voice. "We ship timber all over the West Coast. San Francisco and farther."

"How is the harbor here?" She cast a glance at the newspaper reporter, who had tagged after them. His eyes turned to dark narrow slits. Meredith knew he resented her conversation with the mill owner and wondered what made him so disagreeable.

"Too shallow with sandbars. There's no harbor to speak of along this coast. Mostly use steam-powered schooners now. They get around good, as long as they don't get caught in a storm, of course. You might want to take a look at the wharf where the timber gets loaded onto the schooners. It's something to see."

"I would like that."

"Just a fortnight ago, we lost a couple schooners. Nearly their whole crews went down with the ship. Horrible." He shook his head, his eyes reliving the scene.

"I'm sorry," Meredith said.

By this time, they had reached the wagon. The man, who looked as if he'd be more at home on a cotton plantation than a sawmill, grazed his eyes over the bittersweet belongings of his old partner. "James always did take care of his tools. I'll get someone to come unload this stuff. Thanks for your trouble. Give Mrs. Cooper my regards and enjoy your stay."

As Washington shuffled away, the newspaperman gave Meredith a smirk. "We did an article on that storm. Good day, Miss Mears."

"I'll drop by to see it," Meredith called over the man's shoulder. She saw his back flinch, though he did not give a reply. Perhaps it was old news, but it would make good material for her magazine articles.

Once they were alone, Jonah said, "You shouldn't have set his teeth on edge like that. I might like to work with him sometime."

"Me? What did I do?"

"Just born a woman, I suppose."

"Humph!" She squared her shoulders. She was well aware of that, having heard it enough times in her past. Her father's words surfaced. *You should've been born a boy. If your ma had to die birthing you, it was the least you could have done for me.*

five

The coffee sloshed over the rim of the china cup and caused a puddle on the white tablecloth. Meredith rushed forward. "Here, let me help."

"What? Oh! How clumsy of me." Mrs. Cooper hurried to get a rag, but when she returned to the table, her eyes swept over her guest.

The reporter's face burned. "I should have forewarned you. I plan to dress like this when I ride out to Bucker's Stand, and that's where I'm headed this morning."

"Why?" Mrs. Cooper asked.

"Because it's a man's world out there," Meredith said. She seated herself at the table, Mrs. Cooper's chilly gaze fastened upon her. "I'll fit in better."

"Well, I never."

Concern shown in Jonah's eyes as he watched the women spar.

"I don't know how New York City behaves these days, but the folks in Buckman's Pride won't take kindly to a woman dudded up like you are, no matter what the reason."

"I guess they'll have to adjust." Meredith's appetite left, and she pushed her plate away. "I'll meet you at the stables, Jonah."

"Yes, ma'am. After I've had my breakfast." He was careful to avert his eyes from both women.

❧

"That woman runs hot and cold," Meredith said when she and Jonah left the stables toward Bucker's Stand.

"I hadn't noticed."

Meredith cocked an eyebrow at Jonah. "Perhaps that's because she's mostly hot when you're around."

"You think so?"

She grinned and let the matter drop.

"These trees," motioned Jonah, "stretch on forever. I think there's about as much chance using up all this timber as there is using up the very air we breathe."

"I'll keep your opinion in mind, old man, when I write my story."

"I think I could stay in these woods forever."

"Where's your camera equipment, Jonah?"

"I won't be taking any photographs today. First I need to set up scaffolds that will get my camera high enough to scope the trees."

"Oh? Something permanent?"

"Perhaps. When I'm working I'll stay at the camp for several days on end."

"So today's a scouting trip?"

"More or less. I didn't want you to have to ride out alone the first time."

"That's kind of you. I have to admit my stomach is a bit jittery."

Jonah shot her a look. "Is that a fact?"

A good two hours passed until they finally rode into Bucker's Stand. "Whew!" Meredith said. "I was beginning to think we'd gotten lost."

"Me, too," Jonah said, reining in his horse. "But, this is it. How do you feel?"

"Ask me that again tonight."

Jonah chuckled beneath his thin walrus mustache.

The camp appeared to be nearly deserted. The few men they saw froze and stared at Meredith with hungry expressions. "Guess the clothes aren't working," Jonah whispered.

"Hush. Where is everybody?"

"Probably in the woods."

They dismounted and asked the first man they came across where they could find the camp foreman.

"Bull of the woods? Thar, in that tent." The burly man pointed toward a rectangular gray structure.

Jonah nudged Meredith toward the tent indicated, while she took stock of the place.

One man, whose wrinkled face looked like leather, made a smacking noise with his lips, and Jonah gave her a light tug. "Hurry up."

She felt a surge of disgust. "They'll just have to get used to seeing me around."

Jonah peeked inside the tent's open flap, and a black bear of a man motioned them inside.

"If you're looking for a job, I don't think you'll do," he said. His black eyes glanced over Meredith. "Especially that one."

She strode forward. "We're not looking for a job. We have one. Meredith S. Mears, New York journalist." She stuck out her hand.

"Jonah Shaw, photographer. You had any photographs taken of your camp yet?"

"Mm, nope."

"Well, I'm your man then."

The black-bearded bull of the woods did the formality of shaking their hands. "Josiah Jones. I can appreciate that you've come a long way. But I don't think you'll want to be sticking around. This is no place for city folks. It's rough, and it's dangerous. You'll likely get in the way of my men and get yourself killed." His eyes raked over Meredith. "The only women here are ones that serve the meals, and they're loggers' wives."

"Mr. Jones, we have come a very long way, and I have no intention of leaving Buckman's Pride without my story."

"Staying in town then?" the bull asked.

"And I've set up a studio. We'll be around for a bit," Jonah announced.

The bull shrugged his shoulders. "Don't say you haven't been warned. I'll not be responsible for any harm that comes your way. And I'll be mighty displeased should one of my men come to harm because of you. Accidents happen around here too easily as it is. The men don't need distractions."

"Understood," Meredith said.

Just then, a shadow indicated someone had entered the tent's doorway.

"Talbot," the bull said with a sudden smirk on his face. "Got a job for you. See that these folks get shown around, and answer whatever questions they have, best you can."

"But I was on my way back to the field, sir. One of the peelers sent me with this message."

"I'll take it." Josiah Jones reached out and took the piece of bark that served as paper. "And you'll take these folks. Try to keep them out of harm's way, if you can."

"Yes, sir." The man's voice was both reluctant and familiar.

A dread fell over Meredith. She sensed that this was the one man she most wanted to avoid. Afraid to discover the truth, she turned very slowly.

⌘

Even though the slight person dressed like a man, Thatcher Talbot instantly recognized the reporter from the train and her photographer. The last thing Thatcher needed was her following him around, ready to delve into his personal life. His signing on with this outfit, however, was too recent for him to raise any objections to the boss's orders. When her eyes met his, he smelled trouble.

"No," Meredith said. The bull of the wood's black brows furrowed. "Is Silas Cooke available? We're friends, and I'd really appreciate it if. . ."

"Does he look like he's available?" the bull of the woods asked.

"Come on." Jonah took Meredith by the arm. "Mr. Talbot will do just fine."

Beyond the tent, out of the bull's sight, Meredith dug in her feet. "No! He will not do just fine. He's the horrible man who ruined my hat."

"I what? I don't know what your problem is, woman," Talbot backed up a few paces, his hands fending her off, "and I don't think I want to know. I don't like this any better than you do."

"In Buckman's Pride, the day I arrived, you splattered my

gown and hat with mud. You are a. . .a beast!"

He shook his head. "I think I'd remember such a thing."

"It was you," Jonah said. "But you didn't realize you did it."

"Well, that explains it then. I'm sorry, ma'am. I'd never do something like that intentionally."

Meredith gritted her teeth and thrust herself in front of him, the top of her head at his chin. She tilted her head back. "You, sir, are a rude man. I'd rather be hung from a rope and dragged by my heels through these woods," she gestured to the surrounding trees, "than be escorted by the likes of you. But this assignment is important to me, and since you're all we have, you'll have to do."

Thatcher wanted to take the woman over his knee. "And you, ma'am, are a spoiled brat. But since my boss has given me this duty, and for your friend's sake, you'll have to do."

"Well!" Meredith jerked her head so hard her hat slipped.

Jonah gripped Meredith's shoulder and stepped between them like a referee at a prizefight. "If I were to set up camp for a week or so to take some photographs, where would I stay?"

Talbot eased back. "This way." He tramped off with Jonah and Meredith jogging after him. "I suppose the bull would put you in the bunkhouse with the rest of us." He stopped in front of a long building with rows of bunks so close together that they had to be accessed from the foot end. "And if you didn't like this, you could just pitch a bedroll outside. Course, with the wild animals, I'd recommend the bunkhouse over the woods."

"Are the animals here as ferocious as the men?" Meredith asked.

"Most are." Talbot met her glare, hoping to frighten her.

Meredith raised her hands in surrender. "Look. We're wasting time. Why don't you let us follow you back to whatever it was you were doing. I'd like to see the loggers in action. Wouldn't you, Jonah?"

"Yes. That's a good idea."

"It's not safe out there," Mr. Talbot said.

"We've been through all that with the bull," Meredith said. "We promise to stay out of your way, and we'll even find our own way back to camp when we're done."

Talbot shrugged. "Have it your way." He charged into the woods, not really caring if they kept up with him. They did. About twenty minutes later, they entered a tiny clearing where men were working together.

"By the way," Meredith said. "What's a peeler?"

Talbot rolled his eyes. "A man who peels bark off a log." He looked over the logging site. "You two can stand over there." He pointed.

The loggers gave Meredith and Jonah several sidelong glances. Meredith didn't care; she was too intrigued with the logging operation. Questions popped into her head as quickly as the axes dropped wood chips onto the forest floor.

❧

Talbot looked up once to see Meredith and Jonah tramping off alone. He figured they were heading back to the camp. The bull had put them in his care, so he took off after them. The crackling twigs made Meredith jump. Talbot stifled a grin.

❧

That evening, Talbot lounged on his cot, his arms folded under his head, his eyes staring up at the ceiling.

"She sure is a pretty one."

Talbot's head shot up, but when he saw it was Silas Cooke, he grinned. "Too pretty for her own good."

"Hers or yours?"

Talbot sat up and motioned. "Sit a spell."

Silas parked himself on the foot of Talbot's cot. "She doesn't like you much, does she?"

Talbot laughed. "Why don't you tell me about your trip together?"

The other man's eyes lit up.

six

"Good morning." Meredith smiled at two women crossing Main Street. One returned the smile until her black-haired companion elbowed her, then quickly tore her eyes away. Meredith felt the heat rush to her cheeks. Unlike New York City, Buckman's Pride was a small town. Had Mrs. Cooper spread some gossip? Her writing experiences trained her not to make assumptions, so she squared her shoulders and sought to dismiss the incident.

At her destination, a wooden sign swung from two ropes. It read: "Buckman News." A bell jingled as she pushed open the door. Inside, the familiar smells of ink and paper filled the room. Frederick Ralston, the blond-haired, fragile-looking newspaper reporter, looked up from his work.

"Hello," Meredith said.

"Expected you sooner or later." His voice reminded her of a New York winter day.

"Is there a reason you dislike me?"

His fingers poked at printing blocks. "Just don't like women nosing around in men's business."

An older man with an apron draped over his thick belly entered from a back room. He wiped his hands when he saw Meredith in her feathered hat and flowing gown. "Well, there, what can I do for you, miss?"

Meredith stepped forward. "Meredith S. Mears, journalist."

"My hands are dirty."

"No matter." Meredith warmed beneath the short man's smile.

"Charlie Dutton."

"Are you the owner?"

"Yes, ma'am."

"You have a delightful shop." She made a slow circle of the room. "Mr. Ralston invited me to come and look at an article he wrote about the schooners lost in the harbor."

"He mentioned it. Let's see what we can find."

Frederick Ralston's resentful eyes followed her. She flitted about the room to examine the presses until Charlie Dutton returned with the discussed issue.

"Here we are, Miss Mears. You can sit at that table if you like. Take your time."

"Thank you." Meredith took the paper and went to the designated table. The article detailing the helpless sailors' plight against the forces of nature moved and saddened her. The coast had abundant resources, which, when harvested, would pile money in some men's pockets. Her fingers traced the printed lines, marking her spot. But how many men would die taming the wild land? The ocean's treacherous rocks, sandbars, and storms could easily splinter the latest design of shipping vessel. They snuffed out men's lives in their prime and left families bereft. Her finger tapped her cheek. Dead men didn't make fortunes. Their risks were another man's gain.

Was it the same in the woods? Instinctively, she knew it was. Asa had said a logger's life span was only seven years. The bull warned about accidents. All of a sudden, it seemed important to ride to Bucker's Stand again. She knew the topic of her first story.

"I'm done here. Thank you for letting me read this."

"You're welcome," Charlie Dutton said.

"Are you hiring?" she asked.

"Sorry. It's a small paper, and I have to keep our staff small as well."

She glanced at the younger, brooding man across the room. "I understand. Thank you again, and good day."

"Good day, Miss Mears."

To finish out the day, Meredith compiled her completed articles and sent them off to Asa. Once this was done, she returned to her room and typed far into the night.

⋙

The next day she rode out to Bucker's Stand. Jonah had gone a day earlier to set up his equipment at the logging camp. Once she arrived, she stabled her horse. A mass exodus of brawn and boot erupted from the mess hall. Meredith slunk behind a tree to observe. Two men passed nearby, engaged in a shoving contest and shouting loud oaths at one another. Meredith shrank further around the tree.

A moment later she saw Jonah, walking with Silas Cooke.

"Jonah!" Meredith stepped out with her portfolio in hand. "Wait!"

The two men turned back. "I didn't know you were here," Jonah said.

"I just got here. Hello, Mr. Cooke. On your way to the field?"

"Sure enough," Silas said.

"I'll just tag along then."

She chatted with the men until they reached Jonah's equipment. Meredith's eyes widened. Before them spread what looked like a giant spider web, the loggers being the spiders. Her journalistic mind allegorized even as she tried to grasp the operation.

Huge cables strung through pulleys and fastened to the tops of trees sloped downward to the earth. Several loggers worked to fasten these cables to logs. Before Meredith had it all figured out, there was, all of a sudden, a great creaking, then a terrible crashing noise, and one of the huge logs in the midst of them jerked violently and lurched straight up into the sky. Meredith scrambled backwards in terror, letting out a shriek.

Jonah shouted, "Shocked me, too, the first time I saw it."

Meredith's hands flew to her heaving bosom. Once Jonah's comment sank in, her pulse calmed. She scrambled for a safe spot, somewhere she could observe and stay out from underfoot. A rotting stump looked inviting and removed from the action, and she backed onto it. Her gaze returned to the steam engine yanking giant logs and hurling them up into the air, crashing through any obstacle.

There was a system to the madness. Logs were yanked toward the river, where they would be floated to the mill. Even the ground beneath her shook when the mighty logs rolled or moved. She watched the process with riveted interest and imagined the sorts of accidents that could occur, until a distant physique caught her eye.

Thatcher Talbot helped to fasten the cables. She observed him from her perch and jotted down notes. Hours sped by while she quietly penned words. Once when her concentration broke, she looked up to see Talbot striding toward her. No, not toward her. Jonah seemed to be the object of his wrath.

"Can't use that photograph," Talbot yelled up at Jonah.

"What?" Jonah called down from his perch.

Instead of answering, Talbot climbed up the scaffolding like a monkey Meredith had once seen at a zoo, until he was nose to nose with Jonah.

Another log lifted and slammed down, drowning out the two men's conversation, but Meredith saw Talbot thumping his finger on Jonah's camera. They argued about a photograph.

She scrambled off the stump and to the bottom of the scaffolding, where she crooked her neck to follow their conversation.

"I do have a say, and I say no!"

"Why don't you wait until they're developed and have a look at them. Then you can decide."

"I want that plate." Talbot fumbled for the glass.

Jonah jerked it out of the camera, and Thatcher smacked it against the tree trunk. A large crack zigzagged across the plate. He handed it back to Jonah.

"You can't do that," Meredith yelled.

Talbot glanced down at her as if she were an insignificant wood tick, then climbed down and brushed past her. The touch of his arm upon hers sent fire shooting up her shoulder. She jerked away.

He halted, as if he felt it, too, cast her a dark look, and strutted away.

She leaned on the bottom of the scaffolding, trembling. "Jonah! I need to speak with you."

The cameraman's face was flushed. He climbed down and brushed himself off.

"I need to get back to town," Meredith said.

Jonah nodded. "I'll see you back to camp."

The two hiked toward the camp in silence until Meredith thought she would explode. "Why did you let him bully you that way? He had no right."

"He does have a right to say if he doesn't want his photograph published."

"He did this just to spite me."

"I don't think so," Jonah said.

Meredith mulled it over until they reached the camp. "I'm taking this to the bull."

Jonah snatched at her arm. "Don't. I've plenty of good photographs. We don't need it."

"You looking for me?" a voice from behind caused Meredith to jump.

"Yes," she said when she had caught her breath. "One of your men threatened Jonah."

"How's that?"

"Meredith," Jonah's voice warned.

"He purposely broke one of Jonah's plates."

The bull scowled at Meredith with his black eyes. "Some stories are better left untold. Men's lives can be like that." He tipped his hat and walked off toward his tent.

Her mouth gaped.

"It's not your problem, Storm."

"I'm a reporter. If. . ."

"You better leave so you can get to town before dark."

Jonah's change of topic was like a dousing of cold water, and Meredith's fire sputtered. She backed off. "What about you? Will you be all right here?"

"I'll be fine. I like it here, Storm. Don't ruin it for me."

Meredith's cheeks burned. "You're right, then. I'd better go."

That evening Meredith soaked off her trail dust. It was worth the extra effort to use Mrs. Cooper's rustic indoor plumbing. Water first had to be pumped, then emptied by hand. Meredith did her own pumping, but Mrs. Cooper hired a boy to empty the tub for her guests. Meredith rubbed the kinks in her neck and stretched her sore legs out over the edge of the tub. She hoped her articles for *McClure's* magazine would please Asa, her editor. The soft nightgown draped over a nearby chair looked inviting. It wasn't easy to make the long ride out to the camp.

As she bathed, she recited a favorite verse, one that usually uplifted her in weary times. "I can do all things through Christ which strengtheneth me." The spirit of God nudged her spirit. Why were you so mad at Mr. Talbot? Because he's rude and. . . and. . .he's hiding something. She disregarded God's question in lieu of her own. *Why didn't Talbot want his photograph taken? What is Thatcher Talbot's story?* Meredith reached for her towel.

seven

Meredith awoke to the familiar saying of her editor. *If you fall off the horse, Storm, you've got to get right back on.* The horse, in this instance, was her story. And her instincts told her that her story somehow included Thatcher Talbot. Otherwise, why would her thoughts be consumed by him?

She donned her brown riding skirt and rehearsed her plans to ride to Bucker's Stand and get Thatcher Talbot's story.

On her way out of town, Meredith reined in her horse outside the newspaper office and dismounted. In her haste, however, her foot slipped through a crack, undoubtedly carved by some logger's boot, and sent her flailing. She gave a gasp of exasperation and caught her balance. *Take it easy. You know the hazards.* Then at a more dignified pace, she started off again.

The bell rigged on the door of the newspaper office announced her arrival. After a few polite words, Meredith slapped her story down on Charlie Dutton's desk.

"Read this. You can tell me later what you think of it. Good day, gentlemen."

She strode back to her horse, confident that the newspaper editor would find her article about logging hazards of interest.

❧

Two hours later, at Bucker's Stand, the noises of the steam donkey, falling trees, and singing men led her to the center of activity. Jonah waved from his treehouse studio. She waved back, amazed at the way the city man had adapted himself to the rugged environment and rough-edged lumberjacks.

As usual, Meredith drew some open stares and stolen glances, but she turned a blind eye to all that and put the first phase of her plan into work. Mr. Talbot was peeling the bark off logs. She nestled into the comfortable crook of a low tree

45

branch and reached into her portfolio, aware that Talbot gave her a curious glance. Her back braced against the tree's trunk, she leisurely swung her legs and began to write, ever watchful of Talbot—her tactic to unnerve him enough that he might approach her and begin a conversation.

An hour passed. At one point, Meredith became so engrossed in her writing that she unconsciously shifted her seat and caught a splinter in her upper thigh.

"Ouch." She winced, then cast a quick glance to see if anyone noticed.

To her knowledge, no one had. She scooted off the limb and took stilted, painful steps toward a large redwood. She ducked behind it and twisted to inspect the damage. Her skirt was skewered to her hip with a splinter about the size of a sewing needle.

"Ah," she groaned.

To see the sharp piece that punctured flesh to clothing intensified the stabbing pain. She twisted again, took ahold of the sliver, held her breath, and yanked.

"Ah." The barb pulled her skin and remained skewered.

"Miss Mears?" It was Talbot's voice.

"Go away," she called from her hideaway.

"Do you need help?" His voice now came from just around the other side of the tree's large round trunk.

"No."

"Listen. I saw what happened."

Her heart raced. This wasn't going as she had planned. She felt helpless, trapped, foolish. She twisted around and took another look. Now the puncture wound was bleeding and seeping through her skirt.

"I'm coming around the tree."

She closed her eyes to wait for the inevitable and leaned her shoulder against the tree trunk.

&

When Thatcher rounded the redwood, his first glimpse of her, pale and frightened as a rabbit, plucked his heart. The woman had been watching him for the past hour and writing in that notepad of hers. It was most unsettling, and he had been ready to go over and suggest she run along and distract someone else. But when he had looked over and seen her predicament, he knew he needed to help. He stole a quick look at the problem.

"That looks painful. Did you try to pull it out?"

She nodded, her autumn eyes cloudy, her lips pursed.

"Mind if I have a try?"

She shrugged and turned just a bit.

Thatcher cleared his throat, concentrated on the splinter, and gently took hold of it. "This might sting."

"I know."

"Why don't you put both hands on that tree trunk? You know, brace yourself a bit."

She cast him a frightened look, then placed her palms on the rough bark.

"Tell me when you're ready," Talbot said.

"Ready."

At the sound of her faint voice, he pulled, felt her flinch, felt the splinter release and slide out, and then waved the offensive thing like a banner. "Got it."

She took several gasping breaths. "Let me see."

He handed it to her.

"No wonder it hurt, look how jagged it is."

"You might have a deep puncture wound there." He handed her a folded handkerchief. "Better press that against the spot to stop the bleeding."

She nodded. "Thank you."

Thatcher wanted to get her mind off her wound and make sure the bleeding stopped. He searched his mind for small talk. "Who do you write for?"

"*McClure's* magazine."

"Mm. New York."

"You've heard of it?"

He smiled at her assumption that he was uneducated. "I've read it."

"I'd like to do some articles for the local newspaper while I'm here."

"Don't know much about that. Haven't been here long myself."

"That's right. The bull did say you were new man on board."

"What does *McClure's* find so interesting about logging?"

"Whatever I write will be interesting, Mr. Talbot."

He chuckled. "And what will you write about?"

"About danger, conservation, the spell these huge trees weave over people, about the loggers themselves."

He leaned against the tree, just inches away from her, and crossed his ankles. "Just hardworking men."

"What compels you to work here?"

"Always wanted to see the West."

"Is it what you expected?"

"Haven't seen enough of it yet to tell."

"You going to move from camp to camp?"

"Maybe."

"Do you worry about the dangers, accidents? Maybe there won't be a tomorrow."

"Men need to set their minds on their work, not the dangers, Miss Mears."

"May I quote you?"

"Hmm?"

"What you said just now, may I quote that?"

"I didn't know I was being interviewed. I thought I was just making conversation with a pretty lady."

"I won't use your name," she said.

He shrugged and changed the subject. "Did the bleeding stop?"

Meredith removed the pad and checked it. "I think so."

"Why don't I go get your things and help you back to camp?"

The pretty reporter accepted his help, though he could tell it pained her to do so. He collected her things, resisting the urge to rifle through her notes, and carried them back to the tree.

She placed everything inside her portfolio with swift movements of her petite hands. "Ready."

"We'll go slow. Tell me if it hurts too much."

"And what will you do if it does?"

Thatcher shrugged. "Throw you over my shoulder."

"It feels just fine."

When they reached camp, he asked, "You plan to ride back to town?"

"I don't have much choice."

"All that bumping around in the saddle might start the bleeding again."

"I think I'll be fine. Once a puncture wound swells and closes, the bleeding stops."

"How'd you learn that?"

"My older stepbrother, Charles, is a doctor."

He shrugged. "If you're sure."

"I'm sure."

"I'll go get your horse then."

❧

When Meredith arrived home, Mrs. Cooper took one look at her, limping into the parlor, and rushed forward. "My dear. What's wrong?"

"My leg," Meredith moaned. "I got this horrible splinter in it."

"Why it's bleeding, you poor thing. Let's get you into a tub and see what it looks like."

"Mm. That sounds wonderful. It's so sore."

The rest of the evening, Mrs. Cooper clucked over Meredith like a mother hen, and Meredith let her.

❧

The next morning Meredith's wound, covered with Mrs. Cooper's special drawing liniment and a bandage, felt so improved that she only remembered it at times when she bumped it against something. Meredith supposed it had served a purpose. She'd gotten her interview with Talbot, though it had not revealed much. In fact, it was more as if he had interviewed her. Somewhere she had lost control.

After breakfast and reassuring Mrs. Cooper for the third time that she really felt fine, she walked to the newspaper office. She opened the door in one breath and asked the editor in the next, "Did you read it?"

"It's very good. Can I print it?"

A glow of pleasure crept over Meredith. "Yes."

"You've made them into heroes. The loggers will love it. Everyone will. It's the female perspective of courage that makes the story. It's. . ."

"Romantic?"

"Yes, that's it. Romantic. Can you do more of these?"

"I was hoping you would ask."

Enthusiasm laced his voice. "We could do a weekly column. Or whatever you can get me, if that's too much."

"You've got a deal, Mr. Dutton."

Even the memory of Frederick Ralston's glare didn't keep Meredith from humming a tune. Now if only Asa thought her articles were romantic, newsworthy. He had scoffed at her. Or was that because he was protective? Asa had not replied to the articles she'd sent him. But she was pleased with her efforts so far. She was getting a story in a man's world, a good story.

❧

Mrs. Cooper saw Meredith enter the house. "That gown is so much more appealing, dear. Doesn't it do as well as trousers?"

Meredith answered her landlady in her most patient tone, after all, she had been so kind to her the evening before, almost motherly.

"I don't enjoy wearing men's clothing. A journalist has to do things that aren't always pleasant just to get a story. The readers will remember the story long after they forget what I wore. They'll remember where Buckman's Pride is. They'll recall what happens at Bucker's Stand."

"I understand your point. It's just hard to see you bring the town's scorn upon yourself. I wish folks could see you for the nice girl you are, as I do."

Meredith eased down at the kitchen table, sitting on her good hip. She set her portfolio on the floor, propped her elbows on the table, and cupped her chin in her hands. Her voice took a faraway tone. "I confess, I do care what they think. Two ladies snubbed me the other day, wouldn't even return a greeting. Why? I'm sure they never saw me in trousers. I don't parade around town in them."

Mrs. Cooper's high cheekbones blushed even more than their usual peachy color. "It is a small town."

"Perhaps you could pass on a few good words for me."

"I could do better than that." Mrs. Cooper perked up at her own sudden idea. "I could have a dinner and invite a few choice people. They can see for themselves what a delightful creature you are."

Meredith brightened. "You would do that?"

"Yes. And we could invite your partner, Mr. Shaw."

"He's coming back to town tomorrow to work in his studio for a few days."

"Splendid! I'll get to work on it."

"Thank you, Mrs. Cooper. I do appreciate your concern."

"Save your thanks, dear. We'll have to wait and see what happens."

Mrs. Cooper leaned across the table and patted her hand. "I didn't mean that the way it sounded. It'll be fine. You'll see."

Meredith nodded and reached down for her portfolio. It was important to her to make a favorable impression. In New York, the ladies had loved her. There she was the height of fashion, the epitome of what women hoped to be. Maybe she was a bit of a "new woman." Perhaps this small town wasn't ready for her. Could she fit in?

eight

The town stable boy handed Meredith a note.

She cast a glance around her, then unfolded it and read:

Miss Mears,
   I hope you don't think me presumptuous, but I knew your intentions of going to Bucker's Stand today to work on the column. I have a bigger story that really needs a woman's perspective, this edition's big news. Come see me.
                                                        Charlie Dutton

Presumptuous, indeed. She stuffed the note into her pocket, took leave of the stable boy, and headed straight for the *Buckman News.* That contrary, pale-faced reporter was probably behind this. It better be some big story, if, indeed, there was a story.

The newsroom door banged and its bell clanged behind Meredith. "Mr. Dutton!"

The elderly editor offered a sheepish smile. Ralston wasn't in the room. "I was expecting you."

Meredith wrenched the piece of paper from her pocket and waved it. "What is the meaning of this? Is there really a big story?"

"It's as big as twins."

It took a moment for the meaning of his words to settle in. "Someone had twins?"

Dutton nodded. "Last night Francine Wiley delivered a set of twin boys, and as far as I know they both lived. It's a miracle."

Meredith tried her hardest not to smile. She knew the survival of twins was a momentous occasion. In a town this size it would be the big story. "You're right. This is today's story."

She set her portfolio upon the closest desk and withdrew a pencil. "Give me directions."

On her way out the door, she turned back to the newsman. "You do understand this wasn't fair? I am capable of handling both stories and should have been allowed to do so."

"Perhaps. Time will tell. Now hurry up and get your story before the whole town gets it on their own, firsthand."

"Humph!" The door banged again, and Dutton chuckled.

❧

Meanwhile at Bucker's Stand, an amazing thing took place. None of the loggers, including the bull, could hear often enough the marvelous things that had been written about themselves.

From the groaning tree to the whining sawmill, to list the ways a logger can be maimed, crushed, or killed is a countless task. Yet by use of their brawn, ingenuity, and courage, they persevere. Just as no axe can reach the center of a giant redwood, no words can describe the courage of the lumberjack. These noble men—whose boots tread the carpets of the deep woods and whose dreams soar just as high as any other man's—are out to tame the untamable by raw muscle power and tough determination. Every lonely bucker, every axman, faller, climber, peeler, and bull is somebody's son or brother or husband with a life expectancy of only seven years, so dangerous is the job. I stand beneath the canopied trees, whose roots entangle the logger's heart—wooing dreams and sapping life's blood—and ask, "Don't you worry about the dangers?"

"Men need to set their minds on their work, not the dangers," I was told. And not only are these men's minds on their work, but their hearts. . . .

Thatcher Talbot refolded the worn, now fragile, newspaper in a reverent gesture and laid it back on the mess hall table. When he read his quote, his heart swelled with appreciation. The reporter would not praise without merit. She had seen into their souls. She understood.

Ever since he had laid eyes on her on the train, she had intrigued him, her beauty and spirit slinking their way into his inner being. If she was this perceptive, this deeply moved, perhaps she was worth knowing.

But his life held so many uncertainties right now that it wouldn't be wise to form any kind of an attachment. He shook his head. The eastern reporter had wormed her contrary self into his every thought and emotion, and he didn't know what to do about it. And now, her name was praise on every man's lips in the camp.

Someone entered the tent, and Thatcher looked up. "Silas," he motioned. "What do you think of this article?"

૨**ა**

Mrs. Cooper was as pleased as a woodpecker in a dead tree, doing what she liked to do best, entertain.

"Pass the meat, dear," Mrs. Cooper said. "Miss Mears used to write the society column in New York City."

"How very interesting," Beatrice Bloomfield, the banker's wife, said. "You must find it very dull in Buckman's Pride."

"Indeed not." Meredith smiled at the woman, so near her own age, the one who had snubbed her in town. "Just the other day, the Wiley twins were born. Did you read my article?"

"Well, yes, I did. But we both know that's a rare occasion."

"Nonsense. This town is a writer's dream come true."

"And how is that?" the dark-haired beauty asked.

"Buckman's Pride oozes of adventure, Wild West, romance, interesting people, and determination. I like the spirit of this town."

"As do I," Jonah said as he stabbed a piece of meat with his fork. "I'll find it very hard to leave."

"Must you leave?" Mrs. Cooper asked.

"I'll give that question some serious thought." His intense gaze made Mrs. Cooper's blue eyes sparkle in the same corn-flower blue as the floral-patterned coffee cup poised next to her cheek.

"We would consider you a valuable addition to our

community," the banker replied.

"And you?" Beatrice Bloomfield asked, her brown-eyed gaze fixed on Meredith.

"I plan to return. My father lives in New York."

"Oh? Does he greatly influence your life, my dear?" Mrs. Cooper asked.

"Yes, I suppose he does," Meredith said. There was a general silence around the table, and Mrs. Cooper passed the food again. Finally, Meredith asked, "Is there a women's auxiliary in Buckman's Pride?"

"Why, yes. We have the Women's Circle, which does charitable deeds," Beatrice Bloomfield said. Her thin lips formed a smug smile.

"May I come to one of your meetings?" Meredith asked. "I could do an article on your work."

"Well, I couldn't say without discussing it first with the other ladies."

"We have a meeting next Monday night, don't we, Beatrice?" Mrs. Cooper asked. "I'll remind you to bring it up."

"But it might interfere with Miss Mears's more important projects, traipsing off to Bucker's Stand and all."

"Traipsing?" Meredith repeated in an insulted tone.

"You do ride unaccompanied to the men's camp."

"I escort her or meet her at the camp," Jonah said.

Meredith cleared her throat. "I would not traipse in New York. But," she shrugged, "here in the wild. . ."

"You assume incorrectly," Mrs. Bloomfield said. "I also am from a city, Chicago. And I find your conduct here. . ."

"It is Miss Mears's story that is important." Mrs. Cooper gave Meredith a look of censure, yet flew into a long-winded exoneration on her part. "You see, long after Miss Mears has gone back to New York City, the things remembered will be her stories about Buckman's Pride and Bucker's Stand. Folks who read her articles back in the East won't know that Miss Mears got her story traipsing across the country in men's clothing." Amelia Cooper gasped and put her hand over her mouth.

Beatrice Bloomfield's eyebrows arched.

Amelia recovered and said, "But the things she writes are what they'll remember."

Meredith cast Mrs. Cooper a grateful glance. The woman had tried to defend her, even if she did have a slip of the tongue.

"We shall see," Mrs. Bloomfield said. "What a delightful dinner this has been." She pushed back her chair.

The men at the table bumbled to their feet when Mrs. Bloomfield stood.

"Mrs. Bloomfield, would you like to see my studio?"

"Perhaps some other time, sir."

"I would like to see it," the quiet-mannered banker said.

"It really is something to see, Beatrice," Amelia Cooper urged.

As the group of dinner guests moved outside to view Jonah's photograph studio, Mrs. Cooper squeezed Meredith's arm. "Come along with us, dear."

Meredith trailed behind the group, headed up by Jonah, then Herbert Bloomfield, the banker, whose gait was quite enthusiastic. His wife's hand remained looped through his arm, where he'd placed it, but her back was rigidly straight. Jonah gestured and chatted, and Mrs. Cooper turned to wait for Meredith.

"Don't let that woman intimidate you," Amelia whispered. "I have every bit as much say in this town as she does."

"Let's hope Jonah can impress her," Meredith whispered.

His studio enthralled Mr. Bloomfield and held the others' attention. Jonah explained some of the chemical processes involved in dry-plate photography and showed them photographs of the waterfalls from their trip.

"These are of the logging camp. I'm going to send them to *McClure's* magazine to go along with Miss Mears's articles."

Herbert Bloomfield adjusted his glasses. "They are quite good."

"I would love to take a photograph of the two of you."

Jonah included the banker's beautiful wife in his gaze. "You could frame it to hang in the bank."

"Oh. I wouldn't want to be so prideful," Beatrice Bloomfield said.

"Not at all. If anything, it adds an air of respectability to an establishment."

"Really?" she asked. She released her husband's arm and moved closer to Jonah. "And where would you take this photograph?"

Jonah shrugged. "Anywhere you like."

"That does give us something to think about, doesn't it, Herbert?"

"And Meredith could write a caption to put beneath the photograph. Couldn't you?"

"It would be my pleasure," Meredith said with an appreciative smile.

"It's settled then," Mrs. Cooper declared.

nine

"I see you and Mrs. Cooper are on a first-name basis now," Jonah said.

"I was wrong about Amelia," Meredith said. She hovered over Jonah's shoulder as he coated albumen paper with a silver solution.

"I'm just glad to see the two of you getting along."

"Me, too. Those are great, Jonah."

"They could be better. See the shadows there? I'm still experimenting with the lens to get the lighting the way I want it."

"I've never seen you use flash powder."

He shook his head. "Don't like it." Meredith browsed around the studio. "You working on a problem?" he asked.

"Hmm?"

"Usually, when you get that expression, you're sorting out a problem."

"I guess I am. Maybe you can help. I need you to take a special photograph."

He looked up from his work. "That shouldn't be a problem. What do you need?"

"I need a photograph of Thatcher Talbot."

Jonah grinned. "Lovesick, are you?"

"Of course not. This is strictly business."

"Seriously, Storm, you know I promised him I wouldn't take his photograph. I gave my word."

"He'll never know." Meredith leaned her elbow on the studio worktable, close to Jonah. "Listen. I think our Mr. Talbot is a wanted man. If there's a story on him, it's worth a look."

Jonah jerked the thin paper. "I don't like it, Storm. I like Thatcher. Anyway, if he were a wanted man, he could be dangerous."

"I just want a photograph to send back to Asa. I'll let him

do the investigation."

"And if he uncovers something?"

"Then I'll bring my finds to you, and we'll make the decision together."

"Even if I wanted to help you, he's too smart, too cautious. I'd never get the photograph."

"I'll distract him for you."

"How? No wait!" His hand shot up. "Don't tell me. I don't want to know."

"Does that mean you'll help me?"

"I don't know, Storm. I'll have to think about it."

"I'm riding out to Bucker's Stand tomorrow. I'd like it if you went along." Jonah sighed, and Meredith said, "I know. You have to think about it. Take all the time you want as long as you let me know by tomorrow morning. I'll let you get back to work now."

⊱

The next morning Meredith thanked Jonah repeatedly when he said he would accompany her, although he was careful not to make her any promises. When they reached the camp, Josiah Jones, the bull, tipped his hat at Meredith as she rode past his tent.

"You are in a fine mood today, sir," she said, after she dismounted.

"I want to thank you for your article. It boosted the morale mountain high."

"I only wrote the truth, the way I see it."

"The men will soon be in to eat. You'll see for yourself."

The loggers entered the mess tent in twos and threes, all vying for Meredith's attention.

"Won't you join us, Miss Mears?" asked one of the older lumberjacks. "You, too, Jonah."

"Don't mind if I do." Meredith tried to ignore the stench of working bodies as she and Jonah joined him at a long table. The loggers shoveled in food as if their innards were empty, yet they managed to keep up a conversation.

"Here to write another one of your stories?" the older man asked.

"I'd like to add a bit to the last one, if I could get your help," she gestured to all of those seated about her. She could tell by their grunts, grins, and nods that they would help if they could.

"If I were to ask why you do it, why you jeopardize your life by working at such a dangerous occupation, what would you say?"

"So's pretty reporter women can ask us questions," one quickly replied.

She smiled.

Another piped up, "Don't know how to do nothing else."

Meredith grabbed her portfolio and fumbled for a paper and pencil. She wrote while the responses flowed without pause.

"Once you see these trees, you can't never leave them."

"There's glory in these trees."

One younger man, who reminded her a lot of her step-brother, Charles, said, "Got a mother who needs the money."

"Got a wife and kids," another said.

"Working the trees chases the demons out of you," offered a fierce-looking man.

"It's the smell of the woods," Silas said.

"Came west looking for gold. Ended up here instead."

"Wanted to see the West." The phrase was familiar, as was the voice, and Meredith looked up at Thatcher Talbot. She swallowed when Jonah reached down for his camera and slipped away from the table.

"And is the West better than the East?"

"It's different," he replied.

Meredith tried not to concentrate on his handsome features. She pressed hard on her pencil until the lead broke. "Oh, no."

"Here, let me." Talbot's hand brushed against hers and sent a flurry of sparks through her arm. With expertise, he withdrew a small knife from his belt and began to whittle the writing tool.

A guilty stab pierced Meredith, but she squelched it. "Thank you." She retrieved the pencil from Talbot, with a small gasp, for there was another jolt of physical awareness. She hadn't distracted him long, but Jonah gave her a nod.

A bell rang, and the loggers stampeded out of the mess hall. Meredith stuffed her supplies into her portfolio and smoothed out her riding skirt.

Thatcher Talbot had moved away, and now he leaned against the doorway, his arms crossed against his chest, waiting for her.

She gave him a weak smile.

"On behalf of the camp, thanks for that article."

"It was just the truth."

"The truth sounds lovely, coming from you."

"What a nice compliment."

His eyes were soft like suede; his hair hung in boyish waves across his forehead. "I'll bet you get plenty of those."

"Whatever happened to that rude man I once knew?"

He chuckled as they left the mess hall together. " 'I'd rather be hung from a rope and dragged by my heels through these here woods than be escorted by the likes of you.' "

"You'll do."

He slapped his thigh with his hat as, together, they burst into laughter.

Meredith experienced a sense of wonder at Talbot's personality transformation and felt as if she were falling under a spell of charm. Such magic eyes.

"I have to go out to the field. Are you coming?"

"Hmm? Not today." She patted her portfolio and gave him a final smile. "I have what I came for."

He nodded. "Another time, then." She watched him walk away, sorry that he was such an enigma, sorry she was pressed to investigate him, worried over what she would find.

"Ready to go?" Jonah asked.

❧

Back at his studio, Meredith helped Jonah process the photographs he had taken at the camp. Once they were hung to dry, she inspected them.

"Here, Storm. This one of you with all the loggers would be a good one to show your grandchildren some day. Want to buy it?"

"It's a moment I'll never forget." She sighed. "It was like being the belle of the ball."

His eyes twinkled with a mixture of pride and amusement. "You brought some light into their lives."

Meredith's tiny hand brushed away tears. "And they to mine."

Jonah said softly, "I was only teasing. You may have it."

"Thank you."

"Don't cry, missy."

"I'm not." She sniffled as she turned to the next photograph. It was the one of Thatcher. "It's good."

"Should give you the information you are after."

"Do you think I should send it to Asa?"

"Maybe you need to set your mind at ease about him so you can. . ." His voice trailed off.

"Can what?"

"Like him."

"Oh."

&

Once the photographs dried, Meredith needed to make her decision. Jonah was right. She must know. With decisive movements, she prepared the photograph and package she would mail to Asa, along with a note: *See what you can find out about this man. His name is Thatcher Talbot. He got on the train in Chicago. He may be a wanted man.*

All she could do, Meredith determined, was wait to hear from Asa. In the meantime, she should put Thatcher Talbot from her mind.

ten

That night Meredith slept poorly and dreamed of Talbot just before she awoke. She dressed and went straight to her typewriter. When her wastebasket spilled over with crumpled wads of paper, she sighed and pushed away from her desk. Maybe if she went for a walk, the morning air would clear her head. She found herself strolling up the town's main street.

It was a pleasant morning with blue sky and fluffy clouds, a melodious string of birds roosted on the cobbler's hitching post, and a smattering of town residents went about their daily rounds. One, Beatrice Bloomfield, bustled out of the bank's main entrance, her head bent over an armful of packages. When she recognized Meredith, she gave a start, then a terse greeting before she swooshed away in her chic day dress.

At least it wasn't a total snub. I'm making progress.

Meredith crossed the street, drawn to her favorite store, the dress shop and milliner. The little yellow hat with the green ostrich feather still beckoned from its window display.

❧

Across the street, Thatcher Talbot strode toward the bank, his mind occupied with the news he had received at the camp: One of his old acquaintances was in town. However, his thoughts shifted when he spotted the fascinating reporter, slightly bent and peering intently at something inside a store window. Thatcher lingered over the delightful vision, his back against a hitching post and his arms and legs casually crossed, until she entered the shop.

❧

Meredith positioned the little yellow hat with the green ostrich feather on her head while the dressmaker secured it with pins.

"Take a look in that mirror. You look pretty in it."

63

Meredith moved to the cheval mirror. "It's exquisite."

"Would you like to see the matching gown?"

"I have a gown from New York that matches perfectly." Meredith dallied over her reflection until, with a final sigh, she removed the hatpins. "Actually, I'll need to sell a few more stories before I can afford this hat. But if someone doesn't beat me to it, I'll be back for it. It caught my eye the very first day I came to town."

"That's how it goes, my dear. Once something strikes your fancy, you must have it. I hope it's here when you are ready to purchase it."

"Yes, so do I. Thank you."

Meredith exited the dressmaker's and made a quick assessment of the street only to catch a glimpse of a man who resembled Talbot. *What would he be doing in town on a weekday?* Unconsciously, she found herself trailing after the man across the street. Still unsure of the man's identity, she watched him enter the bank. She loitered, window shopping, and waited for him to reappear. The owner of the general store happened to be sweeping in front of his store, so she engaged him in conversation, where she could keep a watchful eye on the bank.

After a time, the man came out of the bank. *It is Talbot. And he's with another man.* She was surprised to see both men attired in eastern suits of clothing. Her curiosity intensified; a small voice inside her chirped, *I told you he was suspicious.*

The two men engaged in conversation until they turned a corner and vanished down an unfamiliar side street. Meredith curtailed her conversation with the general store owner and skipped across the street toward the intersection where Mr. Talbot had disappeared. She rounded the corner in haste and, to her horror, ran smack into Mr. Talbot's broad side. With a shriek of surprise, she allowed a strong hand to steady her.

"In a hurry, Miss Mears?" Thatcher Talbot cast her a look of censure. The only establishments on this street were a men's haberdashery, a saloon, and a blacksmith shop.

Meredith saw the irony. "Excuse me, Mr. Talbot." She released herself from his grip. "I was just out for some exercise. I'd never been this way before, and. . ."

"It might not be the best proximity for a lady. The main streets would be safer."

"Yes. I'll remember that." Her eyes darted to his companion.

"May I introduce you?"

Meredith gave the brim of her hat a push so she could better see the stranger's face.

"Mr. William Boon of Chicago, may I present Miss Meredith S. Mears." Meredith felt the heat rise to her cheeks as Talbot overplayed her middle initial. "William is an old friend of mine, and Miss Mears is a reporter from New York City."

Meredith detected a glint of humor in William Boon's eyes and had the distinct impression they were making sport of her. Nevertheless, she couldn't miss this opportunity to snoop.

"Are you travelling on business then?"

"No, ma'am. It's personal."

Mr. Boon had a fair rectangular face, covered with freckles, and Meredith wondered what a few hours in the California sun would do to it.

"I'm surprised you could get the day off at the camp, Mr. Talbot."

"It wasn't that hard. I just don't get paid."

"Which reminds me, I should get back to my work."

"Have a nice walk, Miss Mears."

"A pleasure meeting you."

"Gentlemen."

Meredith's feet could not get her away fast enough. *Of all the embarrassing things! What could that impossible man be up to? Was his city friend an accomplice?*

❧

Once Meredith was out of sight, the two men chuckled. "You were right about her," William said. "She was following you."

"Nosy little thing, always probing." Thatcher tried to put her out of his mind. "Let's go have that breakfast."

Inside the café, the men ordered and received their meals. They fell into a comfortable conversation, and William caught Thatcher up on the news from the East.

"After Colleen left, I moped around for several months. One day it hit me. I want her back, and I'm willing to fight for her. I was a lousy husband, but I'll change if I can get her back."

Thatcher sympathized with his longtime friend whose wife had left him. When Thatcher had left Chicago, both he and his friend's lives had been amuck.

"I hope you can find her and forgive her."

"I've already forgiven her. Here. . ." William reached into his vest pocket and withdrew a small photograph of his wife. "I'd like you to have this. Perhaps it will help to locate her. Ask around whenever you get the chance. And here," he said as he pulled out another small slip of paper. "This is my lawyer's address. You can reach me through him."

Thatcher took the photograph and slip of paper. "She's always been very beautiful."

"I wish I'd realized what I had before I ruined things between us."

"I'll keep you in my prayers. You'll find her."

William pushed back his empty plate. "What about you? How long are you going to keep running?"

"Until I can get the courage to go back and face Father."

"He'll probably never change his business manners without your influence. He's only gotten worse with you gone."

"I just can't handle his unethical, greedy, vindictive. . ." Thatcher's voice trailed off into silence.

"He has one weakness in that mean façade."

"It's not a façade."

"He loves you. He's falling apart without you. He rationalizes all his actions. He's meaner than ever since you've left, but there's such an emptiness, a sadness about him."

"I don't think he could love anybody."

"He has offered a reward for any information of your whereabouts."

"He what?" Thatcher leaned forward and his chair scraped the floor. "How?"

"His lawyer sent out letters, inquiries. The word's out."

"I can't believe it. Father owns everything else in Chicago, I guess he thinks he can buy me, too."

"Maybe you should go back and get it straightened out."

"I can't. Are you forgetting Adaline? She's a female version of Father, and he demands that I marry her."

"Hmm. I did forget about her. I guess I was too caught up in my own problems when you left."

"Father pressed for a marriage. He even spoke to Adaline's father. Mother arranged events to throw us together." Thatcher shook his head. "There is no way that I will marry her."

"So you're going to hide out until she marries someone else?"

Thatcher chuckled. "No one else will have her."

William rapped the table with his fist. "We've gotten ourselves into some real messes, haven't we?"

"I'll pray for you, if you'll pray for me."

"Sounds like a good place to start."

eleven

Several days passed. One morning, Meredith started off for Bucker's Stand clad in her comfortable men's trousers.

Just before Meredith reached the camp, her horse stumbled on a rock and began to limp. The rooftops of the bunkhouse and mess hall were visible, not more than a mile up the road, so she dismounted and led her horse the remainder of the way.

As she approached camp, she could tell that things were in an upheaval. Men scurried, shouting orders. With concern, she tethered her horse to a post and went in search of the bull, whom she found meting out instructions with a stern voice.

As soon as there was a lull, she asked, "What's going on?"

"Accident. Don't have time." The bull hurried past her.

"Where?" She started after him, but he paid her no heed. Then she spotted Talbot in the crowd and ran up to him. "Mr. Talbot! Where's the accident?"

"You don't want to see it."

"But I do."

"No."

They glared at each other until the bull interrupted, "Talbot, go after the doctor."

Talbot nodded, gave Meredith a final cutting look, then left for his horse.

The bull gave her a calculating look. "So you finally got your accident."

"It's not my fault, and you know it. I only write the facts."

"Go on then," he motioned. "Go watch a man die."

Mr. Talbot approached on his horse. The bull called out after them, "Give her a ride, Talbot."

Talbot stopped his horse and looked down at her. "Where's your horse?"

"He's picked up a stone."

He reached down his hand and said curtly, "Come up, then."

"No. I won't ride with you. . . ." Her words choked off as she reminded herself, *It's for the story.* His face was unreadable, but he still offered his hand, so reluctantly she took it.

He hoisted her up behind him and nudged his horse. The animal jerked into motion, and Meredith grasped Talbot's shirt with two hands. *Men!* Even though she resented Talbot and the bull's attitudes, she couldn't help but notice how good it felt to hold on to Mr. Talbot's solid back.

&

Meanwhile, Talbot was disgusted with his own awareness of the feminine body pressed up against his. Protective feelings surged up. *Why must she insist on seeing the accident? Why is she so stubborn? Couldn't she just act like a woman?* He cut his thoughts short when they rounded the next bend.

"This is it," he said, reining in his horse. He reached back to help her dismount, but she slipped to the ground and landed hard on her bottom.

She got up and dusted off her pants. "Thank you."

Talbot nodded then made haste for the town's doctor.

&

Meredith watched him go for a moment, then followed after the loggers. Once they had reached the accident, Meredith gasped ragged breaths from the exertion and hung back to recuperate.

Finally, she edged forward. It was a very young man. The one she remembered from her interviews, who reminded her of Charles. The boy had told her he worked at the camp to support his mother. The young man was pinned beneath a log that was too heavy to move with manpower. The loggers had already moved the donkey steam engine and were frantically fastening the log to its cables. She watched the scene before her, wondering how the young man could even have survived. His legs must surely be crushed.

Finally, the cable was secured. "Hang on, boy, we'll have you free in a minute. A doctor's on the way. You're gonna be just fine now."

Words of encouragement rallied around the boy. His eyes remained closed. Meredith turned away, too anxious and nauseated to watch. She went behind the nearest tree and dropped to her knees to pray. There was a giant crashing sound, and she knew that the log had been moved. Still, she waited.

"He's gone."

Meredith knelt behind the tree for a long time, listening to the fragments of conversation.

"Too late."

"Could've never saved his legs."

"Better this way."

"Just a boy."

"He was a good lad."

After a time, Meredith wiped her eyes with her sleeves and, never looking back, stumbled out of the woods and onto the road. She would never forget him lying there. Once she wandered back to the camp, she remembered her horse and led him to the stables. The groom gave him a careful inspection. "He'll be fine, but you can't ride him back tonight."

"Can I borrow a horse?"

"I'll check with the bull and be right back."

Meredith waited, her mind reliving the scene of the accident until the groom returned and found her a mount.

On the ride back to town, the sound of approaching riders reached her, and she looked up to see a dust cloud advancing toward her. The riders pulled up beside her. It was Talbot and the doctor.

Talbot looked at her with concern. "The boy?"

"He didn't make it."

Talbot let out a sigh of regret, and the doctor said, "I'm sorry."

"Me, too," Meredith shivered.

"You going to be all right?" Talbot asked. "I can ride back

to town with you."

"No. I'll be fine. I'd rather be alone right now."

Talbot hesitated, and the doctor said, "I'll go on out to the camp, anyway."

They separated, and Meredith continued on into town, stabled her horse, and even though it was still daylight, went straight home to bed.

⁂

The mother of the deceased young man lived in town. Meredith went to visit her the next afternoon. The small woman appeared strong in spite of her grief.

"I knew when I saw the bull, something had happened to my boy." She wrung her handkerchief. "He was such a good boy. Ever since his pa died, he took good care of me."

"I met him once. He was a special young man."

"Did you?"

"Yes. He talked about you that day."

"I remember," the older woman nodded. "You put it in the paper." She looked at Meredith with dewy eyes. "Will you write something good about my boy?"

"Yes. I will."

⁂

After that call, Meredith visited Francine Wiley, the woman who had birthed twin sons. Their conversation turned out to be as special as the one with the mother of the young logger who was killed. The visit with Mrs. Wiley cheered Meredith enough that she could write up two articles. The first told of the twins' progress, and the second was a touching obituary, which included how the loggers had rallied together to try to save the young man's life. Meredith delivered her stories to the newspaper editor and mailed a copy of the obituary to Asa.

Once she returned home, she thought about the three sons, and her own father came to mind. Then, his words: *If only you'd been a boy.*

twelve

Meredith attended the logger's funeral. It was her first time inside the Buckman's Pride small, steepled church. Though it was a sad occasion, a sense of peace washed over her, and she wished she had attended the congregation's weekly services.

Church, as a child, had been one of the few places her father had allowed her to sit up tight against him. Her father's silent strength, along with the churchgoers' loving smiles, had made it a special haven. When she became a young adult, she had accepted Christ as her Savior.

Today, as the people gathered to bid the deceased boy good-bye, death brought the loggers and town leaders together. Everyone gave a kind word to the boy's mother. After the brief service, Meredith sidled into the crowd that shuffled outside to wait for the loggers who carried the casket of the young man on his last earthbound journey.

The town cemetery was located behind the church. Meredith gave Jonah a thankful smile when he appeared next to her and offered his arm for support. The preacher said a few more words. There was a prayer, and then it was over except for a lunch hosted by Mr. and Mrs. Washington, owners of the sawmill.

Emotional exhaustion wearied Meredith, but she felt obligated to attend the lunch. The townswomen had prepared dishes that were arranged on makeshift tables outside the sawmill. The sound of the Mad River's rushing waters could be heard in the background.

Meredith felt a pat on her shoulder and whirled. "Come sit with me, dear, won't you?"

"Oh yes, Amelia. I'd love to."

"What a nice story you wrote about that poor boy."

"It was a hard one to write."

"I'm sure it was."

"Mrs. Cooper, may I ask you a question?"

"Of course."

"You are one of the town's most affluent and well-respected women. Why do you take in boarders?"

"Because I get bored, and I enjoy cooking. Since my husband died, I've been lonely. The first boarder I took in was a favor to someone. I enjoyed myself and decided to keep on doing it."

"I thought it was something like that."

Folks began to settle around Meredith and Mrs. Cooper. Mrs. Bloomfield took a nearby seat, and Mrs. Washington settled in next to her. Their husbands stood with a group of men across the way.

When Meredith caught a few words of the women's conversation, her fork stopped in midair.

"Journalism in this town."

Not wanting to be conspicuous, Meredith finished her bite, but strained her ears.

"She got herself a story at that poor young man's expense."

"Give the people back East something to read about. As if they care."

"Heard she rode out alone again."

"And she lamed her horse."

Meredith felt a squeeze on her arm and sneaked a look at Mrs. Cooper. The woman's pale face held a taut smile of reassurance. *Should I get up and leave or defend myself?* Meredith wondered. She had to do neither for someone rescued her.

"I don't think you ladies need to worry yourselves over Miss Mears's welfare or her horse's." There was a collected gasp as Mr. Talbot eased into a chair beside Beatrice Bloomfield and charmed her with a smile. "I happened to be there the day the boy had his accident. Miss Mears's horse will be fine, and Miss Mears conducted herself most properly. I think I speak for all the loggers when I say that her articles have lifted the morale of the camp. And Miss Mears was sent west because she is one of the best."

Beatrice smiled up at Talbot. "Well, if you say so, my dear, then of course, it must be true. We do value your opinion." She leaned close. "But you must admit, she does seem a bit unladylike."

"Au contraire. I find her most lady. . .is that berry pie you have there, Mrs. Washington?"

"Why, yes it is."

"I must have some of that. You ladies are the best cooks. Please, excuse me."

The table became eerily quiet until Meredith politely excused herself. She looked around the crowd for Mr. Talbot. He was leaning against a post, staring out toward the river.

"I must thank you for championing me."

He turned with an expression of pleasure. "Join me?"

"Perhaps if we walked down by the river, the noise would drown out the conversations."

"They don't mean anything by it."

They started down the gradual incline toward the river. "And how would you know that?"

"I've known Beatrice for years. She's not a vicious person."

"I don't understand. You knew her back East?"

"Mm-hmm."

Talbot's clamlike evasion of the personal question did not surprise Meredith. "Why did you defend me just now?"

"I only spoke the truth." He looked down at her, admiration softening his brown eyes. "You are a good reporter."

Several feet away, the ground broke off into a bluff. Below that, the rushing waters drowned out the din of the townspeople, giving Meredith and Thatcher the illusion that they were in their own private world. "And you are very good at what you do," she replied.

"Logging?"

"No. Being mysterious and aloof. In fact, I would call you an expert."

"From a reporter, I guess that's a compliment."

"Being elusive is not always a good idea." She gave him a saucy look. "Good day, Mr. Talbot."

ð

Thatcher watched Meredith's not-so-elegant departure with amusement. Her boot caught in a hole, she wobbled, straightened herself again, gave her hat a fierce tug. . . . He chuckled. If he didn't know better, he'd say she'd flirted with him just now. What had she said? *Being elusive is not always a good idea.* Now that could be taken several ways.

ð

"I'm going home," Meredith told Jonah, her voice still breathless from the short climb. "Should something important happen. . ."

"I'll get you," he finished. "Everything all right?"

"Just tired."

Jonah took her arm. "Me, too. Mind if I just tag along?

They had gone a ways in comfortable silence, and then Meredith asked, "Do you think Mrs. Bloomfield is a malicious person?"

"No. I don't think so."

"Then why does she spread bad rumors about me? She doesn't even know me."

"Perhaps you frighten her. Maybe she's afraid of the things that a progressive woman like yourself represents."

"I'm just normal."

"You're a driven woman."

Meredith shot a startled look at Jonah. "Is that bad?"

"You ask too many questions, Storm. I'm just an old man who likes to take photographs."

She patted his dark, chemical-stained hand. "No more questions, old man. I'll just enjoy your company."

thirteen

Mrs. Cooper rapped on Meredith's door.

"You have a visitor."

Meredith poked at stray hairs as she followed Amelia downstairs. A somewhat familiar logger was waiting.

"Yes?"

He spoke with a European accent. "I have a message from Thatcher Talbot." He held out a folded paper. "I'm to wait for your reply."

"Oh." Meredith fumbled to unfold the paper and scan its contents. "If you'll agree to have dinner with me Saturday evening at the hotel, it'll save you a ride to the camp. You can interview me for your column. Please, say yes."

She tapped her fingernail on the paper and glanced up at the patient man at the door. *Does Talbot have a story for me, or is he finally going to talk about himself? Or does he just want to have dinner with me?* It really didn't matter which of these were true. She knew what her answer had to be.

"Please, tell Mr. Talbot I said yes."

"Yes, ma'am." The man grinned.

After he left, Meredith dashed up the steps to her room. She leaned against the closed door with a smile. She wouldn't have to ride out to the camp this week, and she was dining with the mysterious Mr. Talbot.

❧

Meredith hummed as she made her way down Main Street, more to bolster her courage than anything else, a nervous habit she had picked up as a little girl. Whenever she faced troublesome chores, she always hummed.

When she reached the bank, she clutched her portfolio, and entered the building. Jonah had told her that the Bloomfield's

76

always spent late mornings together.

A teller pushed at the bridge of his glasses and asked, "May I assist you?"

Meredith cleared her throat again. "May I see Mrs. Bloomfield?" She leaned close. "It's a personal matter."

He raised his brows. "I'll see if she's available." He motioned. "Please make yourself comfortable."

Comfortable, right, she mused, situating herself on a low wooden bench at the far end of the room.

Presently, the teller returned. "Mrs. Bloomfield will be right with you."

Meredith nodded and continued to wait.

With brisk steps Beatrice Bloomfield entered from a side door.

"You asked to see me?"

Meredith hastened forward. "I stopped in to see the photograph that Jonah took of you and your husband."

"Oh?" Mrs. Bloomfield pointed. "But, it's right behind you, Miss Mears."

Meredith felt a stab of embarrassment and whirled. She gave it a thorough perusal. "It's very good." Her compliment was from the heart. "It adds such a touch of dignity."

"We like it." Mrs. Bloomfield's hand fluttered at her bosom. "I. . ."

"I've brought you something to go with it." Meredith pulled a paper from her portfolio and handed it to the other woman.

Mrs. Bloomfield hesitated then accepted the paper, her finger slowly tracing the professional print as a look of wonder stole across her face. "Isn't this clever? The name of our bank, date founded, and our own names as proprietors. That's very kind of you, Miss Mears."

"You can frame it to hang with your photograph."

"I don't know what to say." Mrs. Bloomfield said.

Meredith felt awkward. "It's just a small thing." Not knowing what else to say, she eased the conversation to a close and left the bank. Outside, she smiled, quite pleased with herself.

❧

When Meredith reached home, Amelia called from the kitchen. "A package arrived for you. It's at the foot of the stairs."

"Thank you." Meredith stooped to retrieve the round box, which felt feather light. *I wonder what this could be.*

Behind the closed door of her room, she laid the package on her bed and hastened to unwrap it. Inside the wrappings was a hatbox. *How strange.*

She removed the lid and carefully peeled back the thin paper. It was the smart yellow hat with the green ostrich feather! *How? Who? A note.*

It read: *Looking forward to dinner. Thatcher.*

Meredith gaped at it for several long minutes before she removed it from the box. She modeled it in front of her mirror. She felt giddy. *How sweet. I adore it. But, of course, I can't keep this. How did he know? What a puzzling man he is.*

❧

Thatcher Talbot appeared on Meredith's doorstep dressed in his tan leather vest. His hair shone, and his face did, too, with the masculine confidence Meredith so admired in a man. Following an effort to greet him as nonchalantly as she could manage, she allowed him to hold her hand in the crook of his arm all the way to the hotel, where they were seated for dinner.

"I'm glad that you accepted my invitation."

"How could I not? You promised a story, didn't you?"

"Before we get to that, I'd like to tell you that you look very lovely, tonight."

"Thank you, and I must tell you that I cannot accept your lovely gift."

"Why not?"

"It wouldn't be proper, Mr. Talbot. We hardly know each other."

Thatcher laughed out loud. "First, please call me Thatcher. And second, when were you ever known as proper?"

Meredith couldn't help but smile. "You do have a point."

His voice dropped low, almost a whisper. "Please, keep the hat. I'd like to see you in it sometime."

"But how did you know I wanted it?"

He leaned close. "I saw you trying it on through the store window."

Before she could reply or protest any further, the waitress appeared to take their order. By the time she left their table, the moment was gone, and the discussion of the hat dropped. Instead, they enjoyed small talk until their red snapper arrived.

"Now about that story?" Meredith reminded him.

"I didn't have anything special in mind." He shrugged. "But I know you can come up with something to ask me."

She cocked her head. "The real reason that I came to Buckman's Pride was to investigate the issue of timber conservation."

"I don't think there's any urgency in the issue. Do you?"

"That's what the eastern loggers said. They waited too long."

"I was offered a job this week that might interest you."

"What kind of job?"

"Bucker's Stand is sending a crew inland to start work on a logging railroad."

"What's that?"

"A track used exclusively for hauling timber. Soon the area by the river will be exhausted."

"Do you know when they plan to move the camp?"

"No. But preparations are being made."

"Do you think the owners of the logging companies would employ conservation methods if they were informed?"

"I imagine each company might respond differently." He sipped on a second cup of coffee.

"Thanks, Thatcher. You've given me something to think about."

They finished their dinner, further discussing the issue of conservation. Meredith enjoyed the evening so much she was sorry to have it end. When Thatcher escorted her home, he hesitated outside the door.

"I probably shouldn't invite you in. Mrs. Cooper was very specific about men callers."

"I understand," he said, although he made no move to leave.

Meredith said the foremost thing on her mind. "I still know practically nothing about you."

"I wouldn't say that. You've seen me work."

She looked skeptical. "I don't think. . ." But she was unable to complete her sentence, for Thatcher had pulled her close against him. Meredith's breath quickened, and she looked up at his face. His eyes were soft, irresistible. She knew she must step away from him, but she didn't want to. He bent down and kissed her.

Thatcher drew away first and gave her a smug smile. "You'll do. I think I'll marry you."

His arrogant attitude brought her up cold. "Of all the impertinent things. I shall never marry you!"

He chuckled. "We'll see, Miss Meredith S. Mears." He chuckled again.

"We shall not see! Good night, Mr. Talbot!"

❧

Inside her room, Meredith pressed her fingers to her burning lips. For all she knew, Talbot was a wanted man. She tried to steady herself as she fumbled with the light. The first thing she saw when the room lit was the yellow hat with a green ostrich feather. Meredith moaned. *Oh, I should have returned you.*

❧

Thatcher continued to chuckle long after the door slammed in his face. He shouldn't have teased her, but he liked her spunk. It seemed natural to admit to her what he had just discovered for himself: He wanted to marry Meredith, even if it meant his own undoing.

fourteen

Meredith's fingers pounded out fragmented thoughts and facts until she came to a point where she left her desk to search through her bags. She needed the article that had first pricked her attention on the conservation problem, John Muir's "The American Forests." His bold words would make a good quote:

> Any fool can destroy trees. They cannot run away; and if they could, they would still be destroyed—chased and hunted down as long as fun or a dollar could be got out of their bark hides, branching horns, or magnificent bole backbones.

Meredith tapped her cheek with her finger. *A bit too strong?* How would the townspeople react? She wanted to get their attention, and this would. She would leave it.

❧

The residents of Buckman's Pride received Meredith's newspaper article much like a hard blow to the stomach. Stunned people turned angry, even ugly. The uproar spread throughout the town until it reached Meredith early the following morning in the form of handwritten notes, delivered by a tight-faced Amelia.

Warily reluctant, Meredith read: "Something is rotten in the woodlands. You!"

Another read: "If you know what's good for you, you'll write a retraction."

Finally: "Come to the newsroom so we can talk about this mess. Charlie."

Meredith's face felt hot. Amelia's features resembled the

sharp eyes of a vulture.

"I can just imagine what those say."

The reporter crumpled the papers. "I take it you don't approve of the article either?"

"It was a bit insensitive to imply that our sawmill is wasteful."

"I only said many around the country were."

"Humph! Same thing."

"I got their attention, didn't I?"

"You can't rip folks' hearts open and expect them to listen to you."

"They'll listen, and if they don't, someone else will."

"You're making it hard for yourself in this town."

There was a long silence, and finally Meredith said. "You'll still be my friend, won't you, Amelia?"

Meredith heard a soft sigh just before Amelia said, "I'm your friend. Just take my advice as a mother's."

"I never had a mother," Meredith said.

Amelia's arms opened in invitation. "Come here, dear."

☙

"Sit down, Miss Mears." The newspaper owner's face twitched. "We've a problem with your last article. It's too direct."

"Caused a stir?" She gave him a ghost of a smile.

"I think every citizen of Buckman's Pride's marched through this door in the last twenty-four hours."

"That's great! We've got their attention. Now we can. . ."

"Write a retraction."

"What!" Meredith sprang to her feet like a lioness protecting her cub. "Never! It's a valid issue, and Buckman's Pride's got to wake up to the facts."

His eyes snapped. "I realize that."

"You do?"

"I let you publish the article, didn't I? Now we need to back off a bit. Let things settle. Feed them some more of the fluff you wrote before."

"News isn't always pleasant to the ear."

His smile faded. "The logging industry is what this town

survives on. You've attacked their jugular vein."

Meredith reseated herself. She clenched and unclenched her hands. "I don't know if I can do a retraction. I'm not saying I won't. I will if it's necessary. It's just that I have another angle in mind. I need some time. Can the retraction at least wait until the regular weekly column?"

She presented an interesting prospect.

"Yours can. I'll do one from the newspaper today."

"Fair enough." The newspaper office's door jingled beneath her departing touch. She paused and turned back to ask, "Did you get any personal threats?"

His voice held a hint of humor. "I guess you could call them that."

"Me, too."

Her hand rested on the doorknob. There seemed to be something more on his mind. "As an outsider, you can write things I can't. But you might get run out of town."

"That's part of being a good journalist, knowing when to pack up and run."

&

Meredith pursued her other angles at once. She eased down onto the stiff chair Clement Washington offered her. Meredith remembered that this man did not relish wasted time. As soon as her portfolio hit the floor, rousing a puff of dust, she began to recite her memorized spiel.

"I came to apologize for my recent newspaper article. My accusations referred to sawmills across the country, but in your defense, the town has taken them quite personally."

A righteous anger bloated Washington's cheeks. "Given your occupation, you are neither naïve nor stupid. Your article's intent was quite clear."

"But, it was not personal."

"Then why are you here?"

Meredith held back her own rising emotions and spoke in a calm tone. "Wasting timber is a serious issue."

"I agree."

"Then you apply methods of conservation?"

"Let's take a walk." He didn't expect an answer. His chair scraped against the floor, and a few papers fluttered up to resettle on his quivering desk.

Meredith grabbed her portfolio and scrambled after him, his words hurling back at her. "Wood is a much-needed resource. Where do you think your paper comes from?"

She panted, working up a sweat to keep up with the man's cantankerous strides. "I agree. Timber should be used. Foresters only offer suggestions to keep these resources from running out one day."

Washington stopped so abruptly that Meredith had to retrace her steps. Her chest heaved as she looked where he pointed. He shouted above the buzzing saws, his finger still thrust forward.

"See what he's doing?"

Meredith gave a half shrug.

"He's sweeping. I keep a clean mill. It cuts down on the chance of fire."

It was one of the methods of conservation she had read about. "That's a fine thing," she shouted back.

They watched the mill workers as Washington pointed out to Meredith many ways that the mill already minimized waste. They utilized the entire tree as it passed through, from logs to shingles. When she had seen enough, they left.

"Mr. Washington, I'm favorably impressed, and I do apologize for the trouble I've caused you."

"I accept your apology."

"Even so, I'll feel negligent if I don't share something else with you."

"By all means," he gestured with outstretched palms, "don't hold back now."

She smiled. "President McKinley has appointed Gifford Pinchot as chief of the Division of Forestry. Heard of Pinchot?"

"I've heard of him. Why?"

"His division offers free advice to mill owners. Would you

be willing to take a look at such materials?"

He shrugged. "I don't see why not."

"Then I thank you for your time. I'll get you the information and put some good words about your mill in my next article."

"I'd appreciate that. In your magazine article, too?"

"You're neither naïve nor stupid," she said with a grin. "Yes, my magazine article also."

They shook hands, and she turned to go, then stopped. "Can Jonah take some photographs of your mill?"

"Already has."

"Some particular shots of how you keep the mill clean?"

"Sure. He'd be mighty welcome."

Since Mr. Washington's mercurial attitude had turned obliging, Meredith couldn't resist satisfying her own curiosity. "You don't seem like a man who would threaten a woman."

"What do you mean?"

"I received some nasty messages."

"Rest assured, they weren't from me." He looked sincere.

"I believe you."

"I wouldn't do anything to hurt my friend's wife. Amelia's taken a liking to you."

"I'm glad we had this talk."

"Me, too."

Meredith chuckled at him as she left. For all his explosiveness, she rather liked the southerner. She was glad he was open to conservation. Meredith hurried home to put her thoughts in black and white.

Yet the dawn of a new day in forestry is breaking. Emerson says that things refuse to be mismanaged long. She hoped her next confrontation, with the bull at Bucker's Stand, would only go as well.

fifteen

A sudden dread filled Meredith. The rumbling of distant thunder filled the air and the shadowing dark clouds rolled overhead like a fast-moving locomotive breathing down the back of her neck. The unfrequented forest that stretched across either side of the road with its ghoulish-shaped trees and dense underbrush appeared dark and forbidding—an uninviting place with wild animals more fearsome than the inevitable storm. She bent low, hugged her knees against her mount, and pressed him forward.

"C'mon, boy," she coaxed. "Think stable." She might reach Bucker's Stand before the cloudburst.

There was a loud crack overhead, and Meredith's horse faltered but recovered his stride. At first the rain fell hit-and-miss, but shortly following that, stinging drops pelted Meredith and her horse.

"Almost there," Meredith urged. "Ugh," she moaned when the sky burst open just as they rode into camp.

Meredith's soggy pants clung to her legs as she swung one over her saddle to dismount. On the ground, her boots slipped on the slick mud, and she slid, her horse sidestepping from the pull of the reins.

"Whoa, boy." She grappled with gloved hands to bring the skittish beast under control. "That a boy."

By the time the horse quit dancing in circles, a groom had appeared to relieve Meredith. "Take good care of him."

"Don't worry, ma'am. We made fast friends the last time he was here." Then he turned toward the animal. "Here you go, pretty boy."

Meredith's body shivered until her teeth rattled. She clenched her jacket to her torso and ran in a careful slip-sliding gait toward the bull's tent. From beneath the sagging brim of her hat, she saw a small lake surrounding the tent. There was no way but to slosh through it. When she threw open the flap, a stream of water poured down her neck and face.

The bull's mouth gaped open. "Land sakes, woman, come in."

"What a mess."

The bull got up from his desk and disappeared into the back room of his tent. He returned with a wool blanket. "Take off your coat and wrap in this."

Meredith shivered. "Thanks."

After she was salvaged with the comforts of chair, blanket, and a warm cup of his coffee, she murmured, "I feel a bit foolish."

He nodded. "You look foolish."

"Know why I'm here?"

"Either to lambaste me or apologize."

"I already did the first. I came to apologize."

"What a relief," he mocked and stretched out his legs.

Meredith grimaced as she swallowed down the strong drink. "The town's in an uproar."

"They'll get over it."

"Why are you being so nice?"

He gave a half shrug. "Hard to yell at a drowned rat."

It was impossible to appear professional after that remark, but she tried. "Ever heard of selective logging?"

"Sure."

She removed her hat and a puddle of water ran down the brim. She wrung it out and placed it back on her head, to the obvious amusement of the bull. She threatened him with a cocked eyebrow.

"Do you use it?" she asked.

"You've seen our operation."

"I think you could do better."

"I don't strip the land clean. We only cut what we intend to use." He shrugged. "But I suppose you're right."

"Have you investigated conservation methods?"

"Nope. I've left that up to you."

"Would you, given the chance?"

"What chance?"

She took another swallow of coffee in hopes her teeth would quit clattering enough to finish the business at hand. "I have information. If you would read it, there might be some things you could apply to Bucker's."

"I'll look at it. But just so you know, I don't make all the rules. I'm not the owner of this logging organization."

"That's good enough for me."

"You're shivering again." The black-haired bull cast a worried glance past Meredith, then heaved himself up to look outside. "We need to find you a place to spend the night. You won't be going back to town in this."

Meredith's helpless gaze watched the relentless downpour.

"Maybe one of the married men can take you home." He rubbed his chin and turned back toward her. "Course you aren't the most popular reporter around here anymore."

"I. . ." Meredith stopped midsentence when the bull jerked the tent flap open to admit an excited logger.

"Got a minor accident."

Seeming to forget his castaway, the bull hunched his shoulders and tramped into the rainstorm behind the logger.

Meredith clambered to her feet and sloughed off the blanket as if it were a chain and ball. She had just enough good sense to grab her drenched coat and drape it over her head before she raced after him.

Through the fog and sheets of rain, she saw two injured persons being helped into the bunkhouse. She caught up to them with a gasp.

One of the injured men looked like Thatcher. As Meredith let her coat slip to the ground, her world suddenly shrank to the size of a bunkhouse, a blur of damp canvas, rivulets crossing a mud floor, rows of cots, and an injured man who meant everything to her.

The bull ordered, "Go get Curly." He was the closest thing

to a camp doctor.

Meredith pushed through the haze. "Let me see Thatcher."

"You can't come in here."

She gave the bull a look that was mostly a flash of raw fear and hastened to Thatcher's side. A blood-soaked arm lay draped across his chest, where a large, jagged piece of wood skewered his coat sleeve to his arm. When Meredith saw the problem, she almost fainted.

"We've got to get his coat off and get the blood stopped." The room quieted under her words.

Her gaze swept over the other injured man, whose arms hugged the shoulders of two able-bodied loggers. "Help him to a cot."

Thatcher groaned. The bull winced when Meredith yanked her blouse out from her trousers. The silence in the room thickened, as the men watched her rip a strip from the bottom of her blouse.

The bull lay his hand on Thatcher's shoulder. "Be still," he said in his most gentle authoritative voice.

Meredith gave him an appreciative glance. Thatcher's eyes closed, his face pale and his lips parted. "Let's get his jacket off first. Do you have a knife?" Meredith asked.

The bull helped Thatcher sit forward so Meredith could remove the garment. Then he lay back. They used a knife to cut the material away from the arm. Next they cut his shirt away, and Meredith tied the strip of cloth tight around his upper arm.

"I can see to him if you want to get the other injured man's foot propped up."

The bull nodded.

Meredith leaned over Thatcher and whispered, "The bleeding has stopped some. Try not to move your arm."

His eyes flickered open. "I feel dizzy."

"Just rest if you can."

At that moment, Curly burst into the bunkhouse. He strode past everyone to a cot, from beneath which he removed the camp's leather bag filled with medical supplies. He leaned over Thatcher and said to Meredith as he probed the injured area, "You've done just right, Miss Mears."

Meredith stepped back from the cot, and the room gave an odd spin. She rubbed her arms and began to tremble. One of the loggers explained to Curly how the accident happened.

"They fell off a stand. Ran that limb right through his arm. Looks to me like the other broke his leg."

A rush of nausea swept over Meredith, and she fumbled around, looking for her coat. But something else caught her eye. From where it lay, it must have fallen out of Thatcher's pocket. She stooped to pick it up. As dizzy as she felt, she had to concentrate her focus.

It was the picture of a woman, a lovely woman. A steel band of dread constricted her chest. She cast an apprehensive glance at Thatcher and turned the photograph over. The back contained an inscription: "To my husband, with all my love, Colleen." When the full meaning hit, the elegant handwriting scorched her palm.

Another quick glance showed Curly pouring some whiskey down Thatcher's throat. Thatcher choked, coughed, then lay back.

Thatcher's married?

Curly poured some of the whiskey over a knife and lowered it to Thatcher's arm. Meredith averted her eyes.

The bull looked at her oddly. "Miss Mears.You've done enough here. Let's get you to a fire."

Dazed, she nodded. Her foot hit Thatcher's discarded coat. She looked at the bloody heap and tried to remember its import. Her stomach lurched. Then she remembered.

The photograph.

She stooped on unsteady legs and slipped the photograph inside a pocket; then she reached for her own coat and stood up. The room swirled, and everything went black.

❧

Meredith awoke to a crackling fire. Her body sought its

warmth, and a strong grip on both her upper arms lifted her to a sitting position.

"Easy, now." The bull kept a wary eye on Meredith as she looked about the room.

"I'm glad you came around. Had me worried."

"Where am I?"

"Mess hall. You still look rather green." The bull shouted, "Cook! Can you keep an eye on Miss Mears?"

"Sure." The cook narrowed his eyes at her, then returned to his work.

I guess Cook reads, Meredith mused as she eased herself closer to the fire.

"Dry out here until I come back for you," the bull said and started to leave, but turned back. "You'll stay put, won't you?"

"I'll stay." She shuddered.

The cook peeled potatoes and ignored her. Time passed, and a sense of normalcy returned to Meredith, so she tried to start up a conversation with him.

"Do the men always work in the rain?" she asked.

Cook gave her a hard look, then said, "Ya. They'll probably get the lung fever, but they wouldn't want to miss a day of pleasure, killing trees."

Ooh. He bites, too, she said to herself.

She turned her attention back to the fire. *The photograph.* Thatcher's kiss came to mind, his claim that he would marry her. *But he can't be married.* She thought about the puzzle. *Maybe he's a widower.*

Before she could sort it out, the bull returned with a tall blond man who didn't glare at her like the potato peeler.

"The Swede lives nearby. You can stay at his house."

Meredith assessed him. "Even if he's gentle as a doe, I'm not staying with him."

The blond logger's lips twitched. "I have a wife. She'd be grateful for your company."

Meredith shrugged. "Sorry. I'm too miserable to think. Much obliged."

A thin, rosy-cheeked woman stood in the open cabin door. "I saw you coming through the woods. Hurry inside. My, it's nasty."

"This is Miss Mears, the reporter from town. She's feeling poorly and needs shelter for the night."

"Glad to have ya," the young Swedish woman said. "You're welcome to what we have."

Meredith surveyed the room. There was a bed at one end and a table and two mismatched chairs at the other. A fire burned in a black box stove, the only cheery fixture.

"Will you be staying at the camp then?" the woman asked her husband.

"Ya. I've got to go back right away."

Meredith went to the stove to warm up and give them some privacy.

When the woman returned, she was alone. "I'll get you some dry clothes."

"I hate to put you out."

"It's no bother. It'll be nice to talk to someone from town. Don't get in much."

Meredith felt grateful for the woman's kindness. It would be good to get her point of view regarding logging and living in the woods.

As the woman went after the clothes, Meredith wondered, *Is this what it would be like to be married to Thatcher? A hut in the woods?* She shuddered, and her thoughts ran rampant. *Maybe Thatcher is already married. If so, what was he running from that even took him away from a loving wife? And how could he kiss me and speak of marriage? I shall never marry you, Thatcher Talbot, if indeed you are not already married.* Then a more poignant pain, *Will Thatcher be all right? His wound could be quite serious if it became infected.*

"Here you go, Miss Mears. You look a mite green. Let's get you to bed."

sixteen

The next morning, Meredith woke to the sound of rain and a rooster crowing.

"Morning." The greeting came from the cheery woman bent over a pot on the black stove.

"Morning." Meredith threw her legs over the side of the bed and looked out the one tiny window.

"Your clothes are dry. They're at the foot of the bed."

Meredith knew she could never stay cooped up in the small, dreary cabin, regardless of the rain. As she fastened her pants, her stomach rumbled.

The woman smiled. "You must be hungry. Slept like a log."

Meredith pulled out one of the mismatched chairs. "There was an accident in camp, a friend of mine. It made me sick. That was after I got soaked from the storm. Thanks for letting me stay over, but I feel fine now. If you'll just point me in the right direction, I'll go on back to camp."

The woman's eyes widened. "An accident? My husband didn't say anything about an accident."

Meredith waved her hand. "Minor injuries. I've just a weak stomach is all."

"Oh." The woman didn't look convinced. She placed a plate of eggs in front of her guest. "You sure you want to walk to camp in the rain? Through those woods?"

"How far is it? I know we came by horse, but it didn't seem so far yesterday."

The woman swept a worried glance over Meredith. "Two miles. There's a path worn 'twixt us and the camp."

"See then. There's nothing to worry about. I'll easily find my way."

"I hoped you might stay a spell. We could visit."

Meredith hated to crush the woman's hopes. "Well, maybe I will. Just a spell." The woman instantly brightened, and Meredith tasted the eggs. "Mm. This is delicious."

The woman joined Meredith at the table. "Are you really a reporter from the city?"

Meredith answered her questions. After awhile, she asked, "You have a privy?"

The woman giggled. "Out back."

Once Meredith returned to the cabin, she said, "Now that I'm already wet, I really should head back to the camp. The rain is a mere drizzle."

"I thought you'd come back with that in your head. It's been real nice talking with ya."

"My pleasure. Thanks for everything." Meredith felt awkward. She hesitated, then gave the slight woman a hug. "Maybe, I'll see you in town."

The woman nodded. "I hope so. Take care, now."

By the time Meredith took her leave, the rain was a mere mist, and the path was easy to follow, though eerily remote. Meredith kept a brisk pace, eager to leave the shadows of the deep woods and reach camp.

When she reached the bull's tent, he asked, "You're riding back to town in this?"

"I'll go slow. I can't sit around here for days."

"I suppose I could loan you a slicker."

"I'd much appreciate that. How's Mr. Talbot doing?"

"He's got a fever. If you're going to Buckman's Pride, would you mind sending the town doctor back? I was going to send someone in."

"I'll go right away."

The bull nodded, went to the back room of his tent, and returned with a slicker. "A mite big, but it'll keep you drier."

"It's perfect. Thanks." He helped her slip into it before she left.

Meredith got her horse from the stable and checked to make sure her portfolio was still safe in her saddlebags. Then with words of encouragement, she eased the beast out into the drizzle. "Let's go home, boy."

❧

Three hours later, Amelia Cooper bustled Meredith into the shelter of her warm kitchen, shaking her head. "I was worried about you, child."

"No need. I spent the night with a logger's wife."

"I hoped as much."

"This morning I had to get the doctor. Mr. Talbot got a nasty puncture wound in his arm, and another man broke his leg."

"How awful."

"Did you know they work in the rain?"

"Yeah." She looked out the window at the drizzle. "My husband used to do the same."

Meredith followed Amelia's gaze and sneezed. "I see Jonah is in his studio."

"Yes." Amelia looked at her with concern. "Would you like to take a hot bath before you change into dry clothes?"

Meredith sneezed again. "That would feel good."

By the time Meredith's bath was over, her body had succumbed to the start of a cold and fever. Earlier, she had hoped to do some writing, but now all she yearned for was her own bed.

❧

Late that afternoon, Meredith awakened to a knock on her bedroom door. She raised up on one elbow and pulled the blankets tight. Her ears buzzed, and she could hardly breathe.

"Come in."

The door opened, and Jonah's bald head popped in. "Mrs. Cooper gave me permission to check on you."

"Come on in."

Jonah entered, balancing a tray of hot soup, which he placed on her desk. "How are you?"

"Ugh. Stuffed up. Got caught in the storm yesterday."

"I was worried about you."

"Got a good story." She eased herself into a sitting position.

"And a job for you."

Jonah straddled a chair and listened to her explain how she would like some photographs of the mill and logging camp, shots that showed the implementation of conservation methods.

Jonah liked the idea. "As soon as this rain is over, I'll do it. But for now, you'd better eat this soup. We're invited to a dinner party in a few days, and you'll need your strength."

"Whose?"

"Mrs. Bloomfield's."

"Ugh." Meredith sank down into the bed sheets. "Maybe I'll take my time recuperating."

Jonah chuckled. "Get back up here and eat this."

Meredith ate a few bites and then begged him to leave. After that, she slept until the next morning. Amelia served her breakfast in bed, and Meredith fell back asleep. But by afternoon, she rose and dressed. It continued to rain, so she pulled a cozy blanket off the bed and wrapped it around her while she worked at her desk.

❧

The next day, the sun finally shone. Meredith mailed her stories off to *McClure's* and stopped by the newspaper office.

"Here's your retraction. I think you'll like it."

Charlie looked over the article that praised the local mill and logging camp for their high standards and told how they rose above the normal tides in lumbering.

"This is perfect. Though it's not exactly a retraction, I believe it will please the townsfolk, especially the part about their fierce and commendable loyalty to the local lumbermen."

"I'm not doing this just to make the town happy."

"Why are you?"

"It's just the truth," she smiled. "And I was pleased to discover it."

"It makes me proud of our town."

"Here are two more articles. One's entitled, 'Bad weather doesn't stop loggers,' and the other, 'Tribute to a logger's wife.' "

"Looks like we've got enough to do your column for a few weeks," he said with approval. "That's good, because I'm going to be traveling for a couple weeks."

"Oh? Where?"

"San Francisco. My sister's getting married. Frederick will be in charge of the office." He leaned close. "I know you two don't get along very well, so this is perfect. You won't even have to come around until I get back."

Meredith felt hurt. "Have a good trip."

❧

When Meredith returned to her room, she started another article for *McClure's* and wrote another letter questioning Asa about Thatcher Talbot. Even with her work, she could not get the man off her mind. She knew that she should not get emotionally involved with a man who could be a criminal, could be married, and even if neither of these were true, could provide nothing more than a tiny cabin in the woods for the woman he married.

But she could not deny the attraction she felt toward him. She worried over his injury. She thought about his smile, his brown eyes, handsome face, dark wavy hair and mustache.

No, she told herself. *I must forget about him. He is not right for me. I am a city girl. He is a. . . What are you, Thatcher Talbot?*

❧

The next day, Meredith still brooded over Thatcher. If she rode back out to the camp to check on him, it would be too obvious. If she asked the town doctor about Thatcher, he might question her motives.

I'm a reporter. That's my motivation.

Within the hour, she was outside the doctor's office. The door swung open easily, and she looked about. The front room was empty, but she heard some noises in the room beyond. He might be with a patient, she reasoned, so she found a chair to wait.

"Miss Mears. I'm sorry. Didn't know I had a patient."

Meredith rose. "I just came to check up on the loggers. How are they?"

"The one had a broken leg. He's laid up and only time will tell if it heals properly."

"I didn't know it was that serious. That's too bad."

Meredith waited. The doctor was absorbed in private thought. Finally, she prodded, "And the other man?"

"Oh. His arm will be fine as long as it doesn't get infected."

He certainly wasn't telling her anything she didn't already know. "But it's not infected? He had a fever the last I heard."

"No. Both men's fevers are gone. They're on the mend, barring complications."

"Good."

"You're an enigma to me, Miss Mears."

"How is that, doctor?"

"You act as though you care for the loggers, yet your stories of late contradict your actions."

"You haven't read my latest article."

"Change of heart?"

"Conservation of timber is a very serious issue, but I believe that your loggers do a commendable job and that the men running the operations are honest, caring men. It's my intention to make them an example to the entire logging industry."

"That's good to hear."

"Good day, doctor."

seventeen

One morning, Meredith visited Jonah's studio. When she entered the small shed, Jonah was putting the backing on his most recent photographs. "May I see them?"

"Help yourself."

Meredith browsed through the photographs, taking special care with the unmounted ones. "These are perfect for my articles." She turned to him with satisfaction. "We're doing it, Jonah, getting Asa some great material."

"He's got to be pleased."

"When you were at the camp, did you happen to see Thatcher and the other injured logger?"

"Yes. They're both doing well."

Meredith exhaled a sigh of relief. "I'm so glad."

Jonah chuckled. "But they're bored. Eager to get back to work."

The way Jonah talked about the camp, it was obvious he was fitting in with the loggers, with all the townsfolk.

"You're going to stay here, aren't you?" Meredith asked.

Jonah paused from his work and turned toward her. "I haven't decided yet. I like it here."

"I'll probably go home before winter." Her voice was distant.

"Something bothering you, Storm?"

"It's been so up and down for me."

He nodded. "The townspeople liked your last article. You should be up again."

"That reminds me, are you going to Mrs. Bloomfield's dinner party?"

"Of course. Mrs. Bloomfield loves me," he said.

Meredith rolled her eyes. "I'm still amazed I even got invited."

"I hope you can behave yourself."

"Mm-hmm. So do I."

ॐ

The evening of the dinner party, Meredith gave particular attention to her attire. She put on her new yellow hat with the green ostrich feather and her matching gown from New York. It was high necked with rows of horizontal tucks on the bodice and around the hem. She smoothed down the skirt, did a little twist, and watched the hemline swirl just right.

Jonah escorted Meredith and Amelia Cooper. Mr. and Mrs. Bloomfield met them at the door.

"Do come in. It's so good of you to come."

"I am so pleased to be invited," Meredith said.

"I have a few more guests to greet, please go into the sitting room and make yourselves comfortable."

Meredith wondered who the other guests would be. When they entered the room, Meredith hesitated and Jonah slammed into her.

"Sorry," he whispered. "Go on."

She took a hesitant step, then pasted on a smile and entered the room. Thatcher Talbot stood, as did the other men.

Why did I have to wear this wretched hat? Meredith thought. She moved forward to greet him. "I am surprised to see you here," she said.

She saw his gaze settle on the hat.

"The Bloomfields are my friends. Remember? I told you at the funeral."

"Yes, of course," she said, determined to ignore his smile. "But your injury."

His arm was in a sling. "It's almost good as new."

"You certainly are looking better."

"Please, have a seat."

Meredith took a nearby chair after she greeted everyone.

When conversations picked up again, Thatcher said to Meredith, "You were my angel of mercy that day."

Meredith smiled in spite of herself. "When I saw all that

blood and that stick in your arm, I was scared to death."

The woman's photograph came to Meredith's mind, and she grew quiet. She wondered if he had discovered that it was moved, or if she replaced it in such a way that he didn't notice.

He lowered his voice. "Your articles have been the talk of the camp."

"I can well imagine," she said. She looked about the room, then leaned close. "I'd rather not talk about my articles tonight."

He smiled. "I understand." His voice perked up. "We could talk about how lovely you look in that hat."

She whispered, "I don't want to talk about that either."

"Hmm, that doesn't leave us much to talk about."

Mercifully, Meredith was saved from answering as they were invited in to dinner.

About halfway through the main course, Meredith's hostess asked, "Miss Mears, your articles have caused quite a stir, haven't they? Are you used to that sort of thing?"

"No. I'm not. Before I came here, I was doing some routine things. This has been challenging."

Mrs. Bloomfield's eyes squinted. "Why do you do it?"

"It's personal. Just something I have to do." She concentrated on her food. "I must compliment you on this dinner."

"Thank you. I was a bit nervous inviting you here."

"Why?"

"I think everyone in Buckman's Pride is just a bit worried over your opinions. . .fearing they might find themselves in print."

"The townspeople are uncomfortable around me?"

Beatrice Bloomfield intercepted a look of censure from her husband and shrugged. "I'm sorry if I've offended you."

"Not at all. It is I who must apologize."

Beatrice changed the topic, and the rest of the dinner was pleasant.

Perhaps Jonah was right when he said people feared change, and maybe Meredith was a different kind of woman than they were used to. She could prove herself, if given the time, but she wasn't sure she would be in this town long enough to do so, or if she even wanted to be.

❧

After the meal, Thatcher singled Meredith out in the sitting room. "I can't let this evening end without pursuing our conversation. Now what were we talking about before dinner?"

"I believe we were talking about what we cannot talk about and how that doesn't leave us. . ."

"Much to talk about," he finished.

They both chuckled.

"I think we can do better than that. Tell me about your life back in New York City."

Meredith would rather they discuss his life, but thought if she cooperated a bit, he might open up in turn.

"As you know, I work for *McClure's* magazine. My editor is an older man and has been like a father to me, helping me get started in the world of journalism. He didn't want to let me come on this assignment. He was worried about me."

"I'm glad you have someone like that to care for you. What about your parents?"

"My mother died when I was born. My father has thrown it in my face every day of my life. He wanted a son. I've tried all of my life to be one. Never could."

"Did you move away from home?"

"Yes. After many years of keeping house for him, trying to please him, and only receiving set downs."

"I'm sorry. You sound hurt and bitter. Not that I blame you. Have you kept in touch?"

"I called on him before I left. He called me a fool." She shrugged. "We argued."

Thatcher shook his head. "You and I have much in common."

Meredith's curiosity mounted. Was he going to talk at last? "How's that?"

"I'm not good enough for my father, either."

"Where is your home?"

"Chicago. My father wants me to help him run his business. He's very wealthy."

"That doesn't sound so bad."

"He's a cruel, hardhearted man. His business methods are unscrupulous. I'm a Christian, and I cannot do things the way he wants."

"So you walked out on all that wealth to travel?" she asked in amazement, thinking of the horrible accommodations at the camp. She remembered her own disappointment that it was not the kind of life she could ever share with a man. These thoughts circled back to the realization that he might already be married.

"Like I said, we're not so different. You walked out to travel, didn't you?" he asked.

"In a sense. I see your point. Can I ask you a personal question?"

"I thought we were talking personally," he said.

"Are you married?"

"Of course not. If I were married, I would not be here alone."

"Have you ever been married?" Meredith saw that her line of questioning puzzled, yet amused him.

"No. Are you remembering what I said after I kissed you?"

Meredith felt as if her face were on fire. How embarrassing for him to bring up that kiss. Perhaps, he was more like his father than he knew, unscrupulous. Then she remembered his rudeness on their first encounters.

She settled on ignoring his question and asking one of her own. "You were very rude to me when we first met. Why have you changed?"

"If you're fishing for a compliment, I'd be glad to oblige. In fact," he leaned close and said very low, "I'd be pleased to walk you home."

She shook her head at him. "You are impertinent."

"You haven't answered my question."

"No, you may not. Jonah and Mrs. Cooper will accompany me."

"Furthermore, I certainly was not fishing for a compliment, and I still find you a very evasive person."

"I was rude to you, Meredith, because you are a reporter. I didn't want to talk about my life." His eyes darkened. "Do you understand?"

"Yes. I think I would be wise to remain wary of you."

Thatcher laughed out loud at that.

Several people in the room looked his way.

Thatcher leaned close again. "You need never be wary of me. I'm harmless, and anyway, I'm very fond of you. See how I'm confiding in you."

She studied him, but did not reply. If only she could read his mind.

He gave another irritating smile. "You don't need to try so hard to make it in a man's world, you know. Just be yourself."

Her lips quivered. "I am myself. And, I believe it is time to remove myself."

She rose from her chair and moved toward Amelia with a fake yawn. "My. I've grown so tired. Will you be ready to go home anytime soon?"

"Oh, yes dear. I was thinking the same thing."

Jonah saw his cue. "Are you ladies growing weary?"

"Yes," Mrs. Cooper said. "It's been such a lovely dinner party. But I don't want us to overstay our welcome."

"I'm only so glad you could come," Mrs. Bloomfield said.

Jonah accompanied the women to the door.

Across the way, Meredith could feel the pull of Thatcher's eyes, but she did not turn around. If he could be so contrary, then she would be likewise. The wretched man.

eighteen

Meredith carried in her hand the long-overdue envelope from Asa. Her staccato heartbeat was only matched by the fast pitter-pat of her boots as she hurried home to seek the privacy of her room. She leaned against the door. Her hands tingled as she opened the envelope. There was a letter and a check.

Dear Storm,

Good work. Keep the articles coming. The description of the logging community is fascinating and the human-interest stories gripping. I look forward to more information on the conservation issue. Jonah's photographs are going to add a special touch. I'm glad I sent you both. Add a personal note next time and let me know how you are doing and when you plan to return. We're publishing a series of your articles. Will send you a copy of the first. Thought you could use an advance. Buy a new hat. Nothing's turned up on that man you asked about, Thatcher Talbot. Sorry. Miss you. Come home before winter sets in.

Asa

Meredith read it over two more times, then looked over the check. *A hat?* What sort of opinion did these men have of her anyway? *This money will go to Amelia.* She rose and went to the window. Jonah was in his studio. He would be pleased to know that they had heard from Asa.

After Jonah and Meredith had discussed the letter from their editor, they discussed their future articles, which would finish off the series. Their plans included a trip to the camp the following day.

❧

The next day was sunny and perfect for riding out to the logging camp. At breakfast, however, Jonah threw a kink into their plans.

"I heard late last night that there's a schooner expected in the harbor this morning. I'd like to see if I can arrange for some supplies from San Francisco."

"For your studio?" Meredith asked.

"Yes. If you want to start out without me, maybe I'll catch up with you. At any rate, I'll be right behind."

"I'm disappointed, but that will be fine."

"Good," Jonah said. "I'll try to make arrangements with someone else so I don't actually have to wait on the ship."

❧

Meredith took her time. Wildflowers and ferns trimmed the edge of the road like lace and embroidery on the hem of a gown. Beyond the trimmings, thick tangled shrubs, sprawling berry branches, and trees that reached to the sky made a high wall at either side of her. Even though she had traveled this road several times, the scenery always humbled her, for she was touched by its beauty and frightened by its unknowns.

Asa was right. She should return to New York before winter set in, which meant that she needed to gather as much information as she could in the next couple of trips. She wished she could talk Jonah into accompanying her when she left California and stopping at some other logging camps along the way. But Jonah might not be returning; he seemed to have found his place in Buckman's Pride.

The quiver of horseflesh against Meredith's leg brought her out of the intellectual world and back into the physical one—of horse, road, trees, and *bear*!

"Steady boy. Steady boy."

Her voice wavered, and she tightened her grip on the reins, but her horse didn't steady. He let out a snort and balked in the road. Then he kicked his forelegs high into the air and brought them down to stomp the ground. Meredith fought to control him; he backed a few paces, hoofed the ground, then tossed his head and forelegs up again.

Meredith clung to the reins in terror as she saw the bear approach. The beast swung his body from side to side and snarled. Meredith's horse suddenly lurched and bucked Meredith hard.

She felt her body slide sideways. The reins slipped loose. For a moment she thought she was going to be dragged upside down, but then her boot released from the stirrup, and she landed with a large thud off the side of the road. Her head smarted and her vision momentarily blurred.

In an instant she knew that her horse was gone. But what about the bear? She rolled onto her side so she could see. The bear stood in the middle of the road, still swinging his body from side to side and staring after the horse until his eyes discovered Meredith.

She heard a groan coming from deep inside her, and then she heard herself say *Run*.

The bear went down on all fours and started moving again, this time toward her. Meredith scrambled to her feet and ran for all she was worth. Through the trees she ran, never looking back. The bushes tore at her trousers but she kept on going.

I can't hear him. Wouldn't I hear the bear if he were chasing me? But I can't stop. Finally, she looked over her shoulder. She couldn't see anything but forest. She slowed and looked back again. She didn't see the bear or the hole in front of her, and her foot slipped into it.

Down she went. Meredith gasped. A pain shot up her leg. She tried to get up again, but her leg gave out. She crawled onto her stomach and turned herself around. Her heart beat wildly; she could feel it in her throat. She listened, and her eyes gave a frantic search over the woods for the black monster. She thought she heard some cracking twigs in the distance.

The bear is still there.

She gave a panicked glance for a place to hide. There was a

fallen log and a large redwood. She chose the living tree and crawled toward it. When she reached the trunk, she sat behind it and peeked around to see if the bear was coming. Surely it would smell her. What could she do?

She heard cracking twigs again and leaned up tight against the tree, its bark against her cheek. Tears made the bark a blur. The animal was taking its time, probably tracking her. A squirrel started scolding, and she cringed.

Oh please be quiet. Dear God, she prayed. *Protect me. Hide me. O God.*

The noise grew closer. She swallowed hard and leaned toward the edge of the tree trunk. A little more, and she could see. She jerked still.

Oh.

She sobbed with relief. It was three deer. If they could graze so peacefully, the bear must not be near.

She watched the deer and sobbed, deep sobs from within. Their heads shot up, and their ears stiffened. They felt her presence. One turned and began to traipse away. Another anguished sob escaped Meredith, and the deer bounded away. Within moments, all three were out of sight, and Meredith was alone.

Don't go.

She pulled her knees up and leaned against the tree until her chest quit heaving. Her foot throbbed. With the back of her hand, she swiped at her face. Her finger caught in her hair. The pins had fallen out, and it was tangled. She must have lost her hat with her horse. She tried to stop hiccuping.

What should I do?

As far as she looked, there were trees. The road was somewhere behind her, but so was the bear. Should she crawl back in that direction? Could she stand the pain if she did?

❧

Jonah arrived in Bucker's Stand and wondered what the commotion was about. Seemed there was always something going on. He was surprised that Meredith was not in the midst of it, getting the story. As he drew his horse up, he saw what the men were crowding around. It was Meredith's horse.

The bull rushed toward him. "Is she with you?"

"You mean Storm?"

"I'm talking about Miss Mears, the reporter. Her horse came in without her."

Jonah dismounted and ran his hand over the horse's neck.

"He's been running. Must have thrown her. But I should have seen her. She would have waved me down."

"Unless she's knocked out."

"Still, I should have seen her."

One of the men in the group was a stern-faced Thatcher. "I'll go search for her." He stalked away.

"I'm coming, too," Jonah said, swinging back onto his mount.

Thatcher nodded, and Jonah waited for him to return with his own mount.

By noon, the two men had ridden nearly back to town, and they still hadn't found any sign of Meredith.

"Why don't you go on to town?" Thatcher said. "Maybe she walked back. I'll double back the way we came, slower this time. If I don't find anything by the time I get to camp, I'll form a search party. If you find her, send word right away."

Jonah nodded. "Good luck. She's a feisty thing, but I'd sure hate for her to have to spend the night alone in these woods."

"Pray," Thatcher said.

He turned his mount and started back. He kept the pace slow and studied the sides of the road for any indication of Meredith.

Thatcher swallowed back the bile that pushed its way into his throat. If she was there, he would find her. He kept on with his diligent search until he was about halfway between town and the logging camp. Then he saw it. The tracks ran off the main road, probably why he'd missed them before.

"Whoa."

He dismounted, led his horse by the reins, and investigated

the area. It didn't take him long to figure out what had happened. Meredith's horse had stomped the ground, then veered off the road into the thickets. He found where Meredith hit the ground. But where was she? He tied his horse up to a tree and gave a thorough search of the area, calling out her name.

"Meredith!"

He'd make a circle and let his eyes search the woods, then down the road and beyond. He asked himself, *What made the horse buck?* If it were a wild animal, he might have noticed it from a distance. He walked back to the road, covering it for a short distance. There it was. Bear tracks! No wonder Meredith wasn't there. She must have run from the bear.

Thatcher hurried back to the place where Meredith had fallen from her horse. He'd follow her tracks. Panic rushed over him. By the tracks, he soon discovered that the bear had two cubs. A bear protecting her cubs was a dangerous thing, even for an armed man, let alone a woman without any means of protection. He and his horse scrambled through the woods as fast as he could go without losing the trail.

Just when he thought the bears' tracks were not going to cross Meredith's, he saw them. The bears were following her. His mind went numb with fright, but his body pushed forward. And then he stopped, a wave of relief washing over him. From the looks of things, the bears gave up the chase and ambled off in another direction.

He looked toward the road. It was several miles back by now. Presumably, Meredith was lost in the woods, probably in hysterics. He had to find her before nightfall. He made a vow to himself that he would.

Thatcher pressed on, following Meredith's trail of broken twigs and indentations from trodden rocks. The area was plush, which made the tracking tedious. Once he lost her trail, but found it again. At one point, when Thatcher thought he recognized a fallen log, he worried that he was going in circles.

Then he heard the sobs.

"Meredith?"

nineteen

Meredith couldn't crawl out because it hurt too much. Dark shadows and creepy sounds pressed all around. Someone called her name. She cried out weakly, "Jonah?"

"Where are you?"

"Here! Over here behind a tree!"

She crawled toward the sound of her rescuer's voice. Her head peeked around from the trunk of a huge tree. Her face was dirty and tear streaked; her hair hung wild over her shoulders.

"Thank God. Meredith! Are you hurt?"

"Thatcher," she gasped with relief. "Yes. My ankle."

"Hold still."

She nodded, and his heart lurched with sympathy. As he reached the tree, he slowly knelt down until they were face to face. "It'll be all right now."

She nodded again and hiccuped.

Ever so gently, he moved toward her, mildly surprised when she threw herself into his arms, best as she could with her hurt ankle. Meredith clutched tight onto the back of his shirt. Her sobs became convulsive, and he pulled her close.

"You're safe now. Everything will be all right."

After what seemed like a very long time, she started to speak. Her words tumbled out in spurts.

"Bear. A bear. Big bear."

He set her at arm's length and looked into her swollen eyes. "I know. I saw her tracks. But she's gone. You're safe."

A sigh of relief escaped her, and she pulled away from his hold. "I was so frightened. I stepped in a hole, and then I was helpless."

"Can I have a look at your ankle? Lean against the tree and get comfortable," he instructed.

Meredith leaned her back against the trunk of the tree and stretched both legs out in front of her.

"Which one?" he asked.

"This one." She pulled her pant leg up past her ankle, but her boot covered the injured area.

"This boot will have to come off." He began to unlace it and gave it a gentle tug. Meredith released a small moan.

"It might hurt some," Thatcher said.

She nodded and closed her eyes.

He saw her pinched lips and the way her back pushed hard against the tree as he worked the tiny foot free from the boot.

She released a sigh.

Thatcher probed the injured area. "Does this hurt? This?" After a careful examination, he said, "I'm no expert. I can't say if it's broken or just bruised or sprained. But it's swollen. You won't be walking on it."

She glanced at his horse.

"You can ride out, but not tonight," he said.

"What do you mean not tonight?" Her words sounded frantic. "I can't stay in these woods."

"Meredith. It's getting dark. We've gotten turned around. I'll need the sun to guide us out of these woods. It's best we camp here tonight and ride out in the morning."

❧

Meredith listened to Thatcher as he prepared camp and started a fire. He still favored his injured arm.

"I wish I'd thought to bring more provisions," Thatcher said. "But I have a few things in my saddlebags so we won't starve." He pulled out a canteen, tin cup, small tin pot, and coffee. He also had some dried meat. "First time you camped out?" he asked.

"No. We camped out between San Francisco and Buckman's Pride."

"That's right. Silas said he brought you over."

"After you refused."

"Like I said the other night, you are a reporter."

When the coffee was ready, Thatcher gave her the tin cup first. "Try this."

"Mm. Good." She watched him and wondered what secrets he harbored. Finally, she said, "So I don't trust you, and you don't trust me. A fine pair we make, except you have the advantage. I'm injured."

He gave her a look of reproof. "You have no reason not to trust me. I would never harm you."

"Nor lie to me?"

"No, I wouldn't. But I suppose every man has things he doesn't want to talk about."

"Like that picture you carry?"

His face looked puzzled.

"The one that you carry in your pocket."

"I'm sorry, I don't know what you're talking about."

"The one of the beautiful woman? Colleen."

"Oh, that." He sloughed it off. "I forgot all about that. How did you know about her?" His voice sounded defensive.

"It fell out of your coat the day you hurt your arm."

It took a moment for that to settle. "You're jealous. Aren't you?"

"How absurd. Of course, I am not. It just goes to show why I cannot trust you or the things you say. I don't believe any man could forget that he carried a picture of his wife."

"She's not my wife. The woman is nothing to me. She's my friend's wife."

Meredith rolled her eyes and shivered.

"You're cold. Let's see if we can move you closer to the fire." He rose and reached for her arm.

Meredith raised her arms to fend him off. "I can manage." She handed him the empty tin cup, then hobbled closer to the fire.

Thatcher made a seat of small timber and leaves for her to sit on by a stump. "Better?" he asked.

Meredith did not reply, choosing to sulk.

Thatcher prepared the small amount of food that was

available. Soon he offered her some jerky. "This will help."

With a loaded look, she accepted the peace offering. It tasted good.

As the night grew darker and the sounds of animals and forest creatures grew louder, Meredith dropped her prejudices against Thatcher.

"Do you have any weapons on you?" she asked.

Thatcher pulled out a knife from a pouch he wore on his belt. "Just this." Meredith frowned.

"And the fire, of course. It will keep the wild animals away."

Thatcher rose and went to his horse. He returned with a woolen blanket. "It's strange that it can be cold this time of the year," he said.

"Amelia says it's because we're so close to the ocean."

"Autumn's just around the corner. We'll stay warm if we share this."

Meredith looked at the blanket draped over his arm and nodded. She already wore his jacket. It would be selfish to take his blanket, too.

He added more wood to the fire, then sat next to her and placed the blanket over them, their shoulders touching.

"Nice," he said.

"Don't get any ideas."

His lips pinched together, and his face looked pained. He remained silent, and they watched the flames of the fire.

After a long while, Thatcher said, "I meant what I said."

"About what?"

"Wanting to marry you."

"I don't want to talk about that."

"Why not? Don't you like me, Meredith?"

She wanted to shout no, for her heart knew that she could not love a man whom she could not trust. There was still the issue of the photograph. But she did like him—too much. She changed the topic.

"How did you find me?"

"Followed your trail."

"No. I mean why you? Where's Jonah?"

"Jonah arrived at camp about the time we found your horse. He and I went looking for you together. I sent him back into town."

"Did the bull send you after me?"

"I came because I was worried about you. Is it so hard to believe that I care about you?"

"But. . ."

Meredith's face warmed, and she felt him leaning closer. His arm slipped around her back. She pushed him away.

"This is not proper. We cannot talk about this now, here alone."

His voice was low. "You didn't answer me. Don't you like me?"

"I don't know."

"You're right. Some other time. Let's try to get some sleep." He leaned back against the large stump and closed his eyes.

Meredith felt abandoned. But she knew that it was best this way. She closed her eyes and told herself that she was fortunate he had found her, fortunate she wasn't alone in the cold and in the dark. She poked Thatcher.

"Humph?"

"Do you think we should sleep?"

"Of course."

"Shouldn't one of us keep watch or something?"

He sighed. "You sleep. I'll keep watch."

"Promise?"

"Mm-hmm."

twenty

Meredith burrowed her face into her pillow. Unconsciously, she shifted her leg in an attempt to alleviate some obscure pain. Slowly, as if coming out of a deep hibernation, her senses returned, her surroundings, the distressing events of the past twenty-four hours, the pain in her ankle. She had spent the night in the woods.

Her eyes started open. It was no pillow she was intimately nuzzling, but Thatcher Talbot's broad shoulder! With a jerk so severe that a jolt shot from her injured foot up through the tips of her hair, she pulled herself upright.

"Ouch." She sucked in her breath.

Her brown hair clung to Thatcher's shoulder. She passed her hand through the wisps to clear the sizzling air between them.

With startled amusement, Thatcher said, "At last the princess awakes. My turn to sleep now?"

A pang of guilt gripped Meredith. He had been on watch all night while she slept. She squirmed into position. "Just hand me that knife of yours, and you may sleep as long as you like."

He chuckled. "That won't be necessary."

To Meredith's humiliation, Thatcher rose and tucked the blanket over her, before going to the fire. He jabbed the coals, and sparks shot into the air.

He must have replaced the wood throughout the night.

"I can't believe that I actually slept," she said.

"I can. You were exhausted."

He fiddled with a canteen and coffee preparations.

Meredith felt a growing alarm. "I need to find a private spot."

Thatcher swiveled around on his haunches, gave their surroundings a sweeping gaze, and strode over.

He scooped her into his arms. "Up you go."

"You don't need to carry me."

"No trouble. Here you go." He set her down behind a cover of trees, then cleared his throat. "I'll go back to the fire. Holler, when you're ready."

She pinched her eyes shut from embarrassment. *This cannot be happening to me.*

When she opened them again, he was gone from sight. She finished with her toilet, and an idea flashed across her mind to see if she could hop back to camp. But she discarded it. Any method she used would be equally belittling.

"Ready," she called.

His impersonal manner led her to wonder if he was going to throw her, sack style, over his horse. Rather, he lowered and released her, and with a nothing-out-of-the-ordinary tone, said, "Coffee should be ready."

The hot tin felt good in Meredith's hands. "Thanks."

"You're mighty welcome."

"For everything. For finding me. You don't understand how hard this has been for me."

"Don't try so hard, Meredith."

She gripped the cup. "Excuse me?"

"It's my pleasure to help. You're a likable person. Just because you have a cruel father doesn't mean others don't accept you."

Her chin jutted upward. "I try hard because I want to succeed."

"Maybe." He studied her. "You are a good reporter. Do things because you want to, not to please others."

"Is that what you do?"

"I guess, maybe I do."

Meredith watched him kick dirt to douse the fire.

"I didn't mean any offense," he said.

"None taken," she said.

"Ready to go home?"

"Mmm, yes."

❧

Thatcher finished packing his gear, then carried Meredith to his horse. "You ride. I'll walk. If we keep the sun to our backs, we should find the road again."

Meredith certainly didn't know which direction would lead them out of the deep woods.

"Oh. . ." He took something from his saddlebags. "You might want this."

"My hat."

He shrugged. "Found it along the trail." He gave his saddlebags a pat. "Got your boot in here, too, for safekeeping."

She gave him a grateful smile.

❧

An hour passed.

"It shouldn't be long now," Thatcher said.

By midmorning, they intercepted the road.

Meredith gave a joyful cry. "This road never looked so good."

"How's your ankle doing?"

"It hurts, but I'm getting used to it. How about your arm?"

"It doesn't bother me much. But if you don't care, I wouldn't mind joining you up there."

She did mind, but how could she refuse him? She shrugged. "I just want to get home."

He effortlessly swung into the saddle behind her, then gave his horse a gentle nudge. "Let me know if the pace is too hard on you."

Her ankle ached at the increased jostling, but Meredith didn't tell Thatcher. She only wanted to get home, off this horse, and away from this man whose arms wrapped around her. She appreciated his rescuing her, of course, but their close proximity only hindered her resolve to stay emotionally detached.

They reached Buckman's Pride before noon. Thatcher slid

off the horse and led her through town, which bustled with its usual activities.

Please don't let Mrs. Bloomfield see me like this, thought Meredith.

Only her eyes moved, assessing their progress and hoping against all hope that they would remain anonymous—parading, as it seemed to her, through town.

Thatcher looked tense as he returned nods and greetings.

Meredith chose to ignore them, her lips pressed over gritted teeth. She gave her hat a tug to shield her face, but it did nothing to conceal her wild, matted hair, and she wondered what kind of nasty notes she would receive this time.

As they neared the bank, she sucked in her breath and sat statue still. A heat of humiliation crept over her. Silent spurts of defense rushed through her mind—much like one whose life passed before them in a time of danger: *All part of the job. Couldn't help it that bear came out. . .Jonah was supposed to come. . . .*

Then to her most nightmarish dread, she heard the bank's door creak open. Meredith dipped her head, and tears soaked her shirt. She felt the horse stop and swiped a hand across her eyes.

Thatcher reached up, and she fell into his arms. She felt his breath against her face. "It's going to be all right now."

He carried her to the doctor's office and paused just outside the door to wipe away her tears.

"Ready?"

She nodded.

Thatcher shouldered the door open.

"What have we here?" the doctor asked with concern.

"Horse threw her. Hurt her ankle."

"Lay her here." The doctor carefully examined Meredith's ankle.

Thatcher backed away. "I'll go tell Jonah and Mrs. Cooper you're safe."

"Yes, please," Meredith called softly. "Thank you."

"Now then, let's see what you've done to yourself," the doctor said. Meredith flinched as his hand probed the injured area.

❧

Meredith's ankle was only sprained. The doctor wrapped it, gave her something to drink, then delivered her home. Mrs. Cooper and Jonah heard them approach and ran outside. Jonah carried Meredith into the house, where she caught a glimpse of Thatcher's face and anxious eyes.

Up in her room, Amelia cleaned Meredith enough to slip her between the sheets.

"You just rest a bit, and when you're up to it, I'll fix you a hot bath. We can talk later."

"I'm so tired."

"Probably something the doctor gave you. Rest easy, now."

Meredith gave a feeble wave of her hand. "Amelia, give Mr. Talbot my thanks."

"I will indeed, and that's not all. I'm going to fix him a big meal before he rides back. I'm mighty grateful he found you and brought you back to us safe."

"Me, too," Meredith murmured, just before she dozed.

twenty-one

For the next couple of days Meredith did little except mope around the house and receive visitors. There was Mr. and Mrs. Washington from the mill. Francine Wiley brought over her pudgy-cheeked twin boys to cheer Meredith. Even Mr. and Mrs. Bloomfield came calling.

The latter confided, "I heard you were missing, and then when I saw you ride past the bank looking so pathetic. . . . I do hope the experience wasn't too horrifying."

"It was. I was never so frightened in my life."

"Tell me everything that happened."

Meredith did not know why Mrs. Bloomfield was suddenly so concerned. Was she as caring as her honeyed tone implied? Meredith saw the raw anticipation in Mrs. Bloomfield's eyes, and Thatcher's advice came to mind.

Just because you have a cruel father doesn't mean that others don't accept you. Do things because you want to, not to impress or please others.

"I'll tell you everything, but you won't faint on me, will you?"

Mrs. Bloomfield leaned forward, a gloved hand fluttering at her lips. "I should hope not! Please, go on."

"I was riding without a care, knowing full well that Jonah was to follow me, of course. All of a sudden, my horse reared up. And then I saw it. A bear. . ."

Mrs. Bloomfield gasped. "I would have died on the spot. What did you do?"

"Well, I had no choice. . . ." Meredith went on to detail the entire episode.

When Mrs. Bloomfield left, she pecked Meredith on the cheek. "Please call me Beatrice, won't you?"

Even Amelia gave Meredith a nod of approval from across the room. Most likely, Beatrice would let the townspeople know she had the entire delicious story straight from the source. It was a thing too good to keep. Being a reporter, Meredith knew the thrill of a good story.

◆

After Mrs. Bloomfield's departure, Jonah helped Meredith up the steps to her room.

When he had left her alone, Meredith did some soul searching. Thatcher's observations had given her some new insights.

Her father verbally abused her and discredited her talents and skills. Yet she sought his approval through accomplishments, the type a son might pursue, not the daughter he never wanted. Could she face the fact that she would never win her father's acceptance, that she should quit trying?

Having never known a mother's love, Meredith craved women's approval as well. Oftentimes, her progressive behavior offended women. Jonah said she frightened them. But when she'd allowed herself to be vulnerable with Amelia, the woman had wholeheartedly accepted her, and now she had risked the same with Beatrice.

She sat at her desk, stared out the window, and thought about Thatcher's alternative. If she didn't have to prove anything, would she still be writing stories for *McClure's*? A still, small voice—one she had not listened to for quite some time—broke into her thoughts.

Don't live for others, but don't live for yourself either. Live for Me.

It was true, she had left God out of things when He should have been the center. She buried her head in her folded arms.

God, forgive me for my selfish groping. Forgive me for my hatred, my anger, my. . .vanity.

She let God convict and heal all the soreness. Afterwards, she lifted her head.

◆

On Sunday, Thatcher visited Meredith with Mrs. Cooper's

approval. They sat in the parlor.

"I've thought about what you said, that I need to do things because I want to, not to impress others," Meredith said.

"And?"

"The statement has some merit, but doesn't it sound selfish?"

Thatcher's brow burrowed in thought.

"Let me put it this way," Meredith said. "I know you are a Christian, but are you working in California because you're doing what you want or you're doing what God wants?"

"You ask some tough questions."

The room grew silent.

Finally, he said, "Both, I think."

She lifted her injured foot to illustrate her point. "I've had plenty of time to do some serious soul searching. What I'm trying to say is I was seeking the praise of others. I don't want to do that anymore. But neither do I want to indulge my own selfish desires. I need to live for God."

"That's admirable," Thatcher said.

"Do you think so? You're serious about your faith?"

"Of course, I am. Your question about selfish motives gives me something to think about."

They smiled and gazed at each other, neither quite knowing what to say. It was one of those moments when souls mesh.

"Maybe we can help each other," he said.

She cocked her head. "What do you mean?"

"As Christians."

"Oh."

Thatcher fiddled with his hat, which lay across his knee. "I've been thinking I should go to church. I miss it."

"Me, too."

"See there. We've helped each other already."

Meredith wondered if she should ask him again about the photograph of the woman. Would he tell her why he didn't want Jonah to take his photograph? If only she could trust him. She didn't want to ruin the special moment. Instead, she asked, "Do you think you'll ever go back to Chicago?"

"Perhaps someday. I'd have to be ready to make things right with Father."

"When I go home, I'll apologize to my father." She sighed. "Not that it will do any good. I'll put aside my expectations."

"Do you have plans to return?"

"Asa, my editor, wants me to return before winter."

Thatcher grew pensive.

&

That evening after Thatcher was gone, Amelia brought a sealed envelope to Meredith's room. "A message boy brought this."

"Thanks." Hesitant, not knowing what to expect, Meredith opened it and read: "Stories circulate around town. We think you're a tramp. Go back to New York where you belong."

Meredith gasped, and Amelia, who had waited by the door, stepped into her room with concern. "What is it, dear? Bad news?"

Disappointed and hurt, Meredith handed Amelia the paper. The older woman's eyes quickly scanned the contents.

"This is outrageous! Whoever wrote such a thing is the one that needs to leave town. Don't you worry yourself about this demented person, whoever he is."

"He?" Meredith murmured.

Amelia calmed. "That's the bad thing about someone who does things backhandedly. It makes you crazy trying to guess who did it. But we shouldn't accuse anyone. It's probably not at all who we think it might be."

Meredith nodded. Journalism demanded evidence. "Could you look in that bag for my Bible?"

"Surely, I can." Amelia's hips swayed determinedly as she crossed the room. Her lips pinched, she searched for the book. "Here you go, dear." She hovered over Meredith. "I'll run along, but I'll check on you before I go to bed."

Meredith clung to her Bible and nodded.

Amelia tiptoed from the room as if she treaded on holy ground.

twenty-two

The following Saturday evening, Thatcher rode into Buckman's Pride, got a room at the hotel, and ordered a bath. After he shaved, he wrestled back his wavy hair, donned his best tan leather vest, brown pants, and boots. The hotel provided him with a hot, tasty dinner of clam chowder and fried chicken. Once his stomach was full, he started out for Mrs. Cooper's.

Meredith's plans to leave California before winter pressed him with an urgency to do some serious courting. After that, he would propose, only properly this time. He chuckled over the memory of his last one, feeble as it was. She sure was pretty when she got mad. He would start his new courting campaign with an invitation to attend church with him tomorrow.

As he walked, the setting sun provided enough light for Thatcher to admire a carefully landscaped yard, which included a flower garden. Overcome with a sudden romantic urge, he plucked a handful of flowers. He would do things properly tonight.

❧

Mrs. Cooper answered the door, took one look at the bouquet, and gave Thatcher a conspiratorial smile.

"Mr. Talbot. What a pleasant surprise. Come in."

"Is Miss Mears at home?"

"Yes, she is. She's in the sitting room. Go on in."

With his bouquet of flowers held just so, Thatcher went to the parlor. He entered with a confident step. He opened his mouth to greet Meredith, but quickly snapped it closed.

On the sofa sat a prettily posed Meredith, a man pressed up against her.

Thatcher clenched his fists and felt the flower stems snap.

Meredith stared at him, her eyes going from his face to the

125

sagging bouquet and back to his face.

Finally she said, "Mr. Talbot."

Thatcher did not miss the use of his formal name nor the uncertainty in her tone of voice. He couldn't even reply.

Meredith stumbled to her feet. The man beside her lurched forward, offering Meredith his arm. They stood there, staring at him, she with her vulnerable expression, the man with his hand supporting Meredith's elbow.

"Thatcher, I'd like you to meet Charles."

A quiver flicked Thatcher's cheek. He bumbled forward, awkwardly sticking out his hand. The man introduced as Charles looked at the flowers thrust out at him. Thatcher snatched his hand back and offered the other one. "How do."

"Pleased to meet you," Charles said.

Is he going to give me the flowers or not? I've never seen Thatcher act so strange. This is beginning to get awkward.

"Let's all sit down," she said with stilted friendliness.

"No. I have to go." Thatcher gave a small nod, turned on his boot heels, and fled from the room.

Meredith took a few steps after him, her mouth agape.

The outer door banged.

"What was that all about?" Charles asked.

"I'm not sure," Meredith said. She turned back to Charles. "I think you scared him off. He's either very jealous or very mad about now."

"Why didn't you tell him I was your brother?"

Meredith's hand clasped over her mouth. "I bumbled that, didn't I?"

"Do you want me to go after him?" her stepbrother asked.

"No. It's better this way."

The two settled back onto the sofa. "Want to tell me about him?"

"I think I'm falling in love," she said.

"Mm." Charles's eyes narrowed. "Father was right to be worried about you."

"I still cannot believe that Father cares anything about me."

"He does. I know he doesn't show it. But when you left, it crushed him. He said it was like losing your mother all over again. He broke down and cried, begged me to come after you."

"I'm frightened. It's what I've always wanted, but now I'm afraid to face him."

"It will take time and patience."

"Do you think he'll get angry when he finds out I'm not coming right home with you?"

Charles shrugged thoughtfully. "I don't know."

"I have to finish this story."

He patted her hand. "Do what you have to do, sister."

⁂

Back in his hotel room, Thatcher plopped on the bed, his arms behind his head, and glared at the ceiling. What a cold-hearted woman. How dare she question him about the picture in his pocket when all of the time she had a gentleman friend in New York City?

What a fool he had made of himself. If it was the last thing he ever accomplished, he would wipe the memory of that traitorous woman from his mind. He had come to town to attend church services. Maybe God was stopping him from making a terrible mistake.

⁂

Meredith dressed carefully for her first church service. She would wear the yellow hat. It was by far her favorite, and if by chance Thatcher showed, maybe it would encourage him. She hadn't meant to embarrass or hurt him. If only she could get a chance to explain about her stepbrother and clear up the misunderstanding.

When Meredith arrived at church, heads nearly jerked off necks, twisting to get a better look at her and the stranger. She couldn't help but wonder if anyone seated in the pews had sent her that nasty message. But she quickly cast the thought aside, for God's house was certainly not the place to harbor grudges. When she let it go, a peace settled over her.

Mrs. Bloomfield turned from the pew in front of Meredith. "Good morning, Miss Mears."

"Good morning." Meredith leaned forward with a smile. "Mrs. Bloomfield, this is my stepbrother, visiting from New York. His name is Charles Mears."

"Welcome to our church, Mr. Mears. It is good to have you." She gave Meredith a flashing smile and turned back.

After the service, the congregation disassembled, and Meredith noticed Thatcher fidgeting. He was blocked in the pew, wearing the expression of a frightened bird. If she hurried, she might be able to reach him before he flew the coop. She tugged Charles's coat sleeve.

"Come along."

Meredith felt her stepbrother's hesitation, but gave another tug. This time he followed.

When he saw where they were headed, he whispered, "Don't do it, Meredith."

She turned to Charles with frustration. "I just want to explain. It isn't right to leave Thatcher thinking. . .you know."

"But you told me you have suspicions about him," Charles whispered. "I can't let my sister throw herself at someone who isn't worthy."

"Nonsense." She released his arm and turned away. But when she did, the pew where Thatcher had been standing was empty. She shot an angry glance back at Charles and hurried down the aisle toward the door.

"Miss Mears," Mrs. Bloomfield said, "everyone is waiting for you to introduce your stepbrother."

Meredith's spirits sagged. "Of course." She waited for Charles to join her, and by the time they exited the church, Thatcher Talbot was nowhere in sight.

twenty-three

Meredith met Jonah in the upstairs hallway. "Oh, Jonah. I need to talk to you."

"I was going down to breakfast. You?"

"Yes, I was. But I wanted to speak with you privately."

Jonah leaned against the wall. "What's on your mind, Storm?"

"I'm making plans to return to New York in September. I hope to visit one or two other logging camps during the time I have left. Are you returning with me, or do you have your own plans?"

Jonah's boot drew involuntary circles on the floor. "I'd like to stay through the winter at least, maybe longer." He looked up at her. "But don't you worry. We'll find someone to travel with you. I won't let you down."

"That's just it. Charles has offered to come back for me. I need to give him my answer by tomorrow."

Jonah's face lit. "That'll work out fine, then, won't it?"

"I'll miss you."

He gave her a brotherly hug. "This whole town'll miss you."

"Let's go get breakfast."

During the meal, Meredith discussed travel plans with her stepbrother. They would spend a couple of weeks visiting other camps, then take the train from San Francisco to the East. She had a month to finish her business in Buckman's Pride.

≈

The following day, Meredith saw her brother off, then went to the newspaper office. Her ankle felt completely healed, and the sun made the walk pleasant. She hoped the editor would be back in town. She had not heard anything of him since her accident.

Ralston bristled at her entrance.

"Is Charlie back yet?"

"Nope."

"When do you expect him?"

"Don't know."

"Really?" She placed her hands on her hips, knowing full well that Ralston would not have been left in charge of the newspaper without knowing when Charlie was returning or without knowing Charlie's tentative plans.

Before she could utter a reply, however, the newsroom's front door flew open, and the bell clanged as the door hit the wall. Meredith jumped and turned.

There stood Thatcher Talbot, his eyes furious. "I'd have a word with you," he said.

She squared her shoulders. "If you can wait one moment." She turned back to Ralston.

Thatcher, however, ignored her request and covered the few steps between them. "Why did you lie to me?"

"I did no such thing." By this time, the reporter across the room was on the edge of his seat.

"Why didn't you tell me he was your stepbrother? You led me to believe he was a suitor!"

"You did not give me a chance to explain." She looked back at Ralston, who had a smile plastered across his frail face. "Mr. Talbot, may we please go someplace private to continue this discussion?"

"You want to take it on the street?"

She glared at him. "May we use the back room, Ralston?"

"By all means. Don't break anything," the reporter said.

Meredith stomped past him and into the back room. Thatcher followed and closed the door. "You should have told me he was your brother," he repeated.

"I'm sorry. When I saw you there with those flowers, I was so stunned that I made an awkward introduction. If you'd stayed around, I would have explained."

He splayed his arms. "How could I know?"

Meredith heaved a great sigh. "I tried to reach you in church, Sunday, to explain, but you rushed out." She earnestly appealed. "I'm really sorry."

He shook his head. "You have no idea how humiliated, how furious I have been at you."

"Charles is my father's first wife's son. My father adopted him. Just so you know all, Charles is returning for me in September."

This news doused him like a canteen of icy water from the Mad River, and Thatcher instantly softened. "I'm only thankful that Beatrice told me when she did. Otherwise, I might have wasted these last few weeks. I'm sorry for embarrassing you in front of that reporter out there."

At the thought of the gloating reporter in the other room, Meredith said, "We'd better go if you feel things are settled now."

Thatcher opened the door. It was an awkward moment.

Meredith made stiff strides across the newsroom, Thatcher right behind her. At the door she turned back.

"Let me know when the editor returns to town."

Ralston saluted her.

Outside, Thatcher gently took her arm. "I've got to get back to the camp. I was doing some banking for the bull. That's how I found out."

"I understand."

"May I call on Saturday night?"

"Oh, Thatcher, I don't know."

"Please."

"Do as you think best."

"Saturday night then." With a big reckless grin that melted her heart, he tipped his hat.

ॐ

Back at the newspaper office, Ralston was having a glorious time, typing furiously. This spoof would catch the town's attention. *Town reporter caught in lie. Hero duped by stepbrother, wishes he had left reporter for bear meat.*

੩

A few days later, a storm flew into the same newspaper office. The door clanged, and the bell vibrated.

Meredith halted.

"You're back! High time!" She slapped a copy of the newspaper down on the editor-in-chief's desk. "Can you tell me the meaning of this?"

"I was just discussing this with Frederick." Ralston only looked amused, rather like a cat savoring a mouse.

Meredith's lower lip trembled with indignation. "Is this how you allow your reporters to be treated? Haven't I experienced enough humiliation in this town without getting stabbed in the back by this paper?"

The editor-in-chief looked at Ralston. "What have you to say to that?"

He shrugged his shoulders. "It was a spoof. Everyone knows that. Can't you take a joke, Miss Mears?"

"You made me out to be a liar. You know what that can do to the credibility of a journalist. I want a retraction."

"And you'll get one," the editor soothed.

Cold steely eyes bored into him from the other desk.

Meredith walked over to Ralston. "You'd better make it sweet, if you know what's good for you."

"Is that a threat, Miss Mears?"

The editor-in-chief pushed back his chair. "That will be enough. I'm sick of this childishness." He cast angry eyes on the male reporter. "You've work to do," and then back on Meredith, "I'll see you another day, when you've cooled down."

Meredith stalked out of the office. Her head stooped, she marched down Main Street.

"Miss Mears!" A feminine voice beckoned from across the street. "Please, wait."

Meredith stopped. *Not now!* The adrenaline still boiled her blood. It was Beatrice Bloomfield. Meredith swallowed hard, then turned to wait. She concentrated on giving a calm, steady greeting.

"I am so sorry for the trouble I've caused," Beatrice said with all earnestness. "I never meant to harm you, dear. Please. Come over for some tea. Let me explain."

"That isn't necessary."

"But my dear friend, I must."

The "dear friend" drew Meredith, and she nodded.

The other woman took Meredith's arm and led her back across the street and into the house that was situated just around the corner from the bank.

They entered the parlor where Beatrice had received her guests the night of her dinner party. Meredith took a seat on one of the mahogany chairs and stared down at the floral rug while she struggled for composure. Beatrice prepared their tea.

When Beatrice returned to the room, she said, "Thatcher Talbot is a dear friend of our family. I probably shouldn't tell you this, but he's quite taken with you. He was the one who helped me to understand you and. . .well, I wasn't very kind to you at first." Her eyes became pools of regret.

"He did?"

"Yes. After that, I discovered for myself you are a fine person. It was my own fears that gave me such a bad start with you. Will you forgive me?"

Meredith set aside her cup and gave Beatrice a sincere smile. "Of course, I shall. It was my fault, too. I'm much too forceful, and too vain, and. . ."

"Do stop. There's more. I've messed things up badly. I mentioned your stepbrother to Thatcher. By the way he stormed out of the bank, I know I got you in trouble."

Meredith giggled. "I am glad he didn't have an axe in his hand that day."

Beatrice smiled. "I think Mr. Ralston must have it in for you."

"His male pride, my female pride. I'm so ashamed. I just came from the newsroom where I blasted all of them."

"Oh, my."

"Yes. I think I need to go home and pray."

"As do we all."

⋰

By evening, Meredith felt much recovered. After supper, Meredith and Jonah lingered companionably at the table with their coffee. Amelia wiped her hands on her apron, gave a nervous smile, and then went to the cupboard.

When she returned, she mumbled sorrowfully, "Another message," and snapped it on the table, where they all stared at it as if it were some evil thing.

Meredith's good spirits wilted. "You read it, Jonah."

His eyes scanned the note. "It's most unpleasant." He shook his head. "I can't do it, Storm."

"Please. Go on."

His baritone held distaste: " 'A tramp and a liar. What other traits may we look forward to? You're a disgrace to Buckman's Pride. Move on.' Don't pay any attention to this," Jonah urged.

"I think it's time that we find out who this troublemaker is," Amelia said.

"How?" Jonah asked.

"It was the same delivery boy. He wouldn't talk to me, just ran off. But if we confront him in front of his mama, the lad might speak."

"I'll go tomorrow," Jonah said.

"I know his mama. I'll go along."

"We'll all go. You're such good friends." Meredith said. "I think I'll go to my room."

"Good night, dear." Amelia gave an effort at cheerfulness.

In the privacy of her room, Meredith took out her Bible. She was learning that God could sustain her through hard times.

twenty-four

Inside the mess hall at Bucker's Stand, Thatcher bent over his meal, chewing but not tasting, as the conversation around the table grew more and more annoying.

"We saw what was happening between you and that reporter."

"Be blind not to."

"Not that we blame you. Never saw a prettier girl."

"I want to know what you was thinking, cozyin' up to a reporter."

"Maybe he wanted to make the news."

"Sure way to do it, courting a reporter."

"It might be worth a night in the woods alone."

"This the only tree you men can climb?" Silas growled.

"She's got a spell cast over you, too."

"Her spell is over all of you, if you'd only admit it," he replied back.

Thatcher didn't mind so much that he was the camp's joke, nor care much if anyone came to his defense or not. What worried him was what Ralston's spoof would do to his and Meredith's relationship. Would she pack up her bags and leave? What if she left town without a word to him?

He was glad tomorrow was Saturday. Otherwise, he'd forget about work and ride into town today. But one more day shouldn't matter that much. If she was gone, then. . .then maybe it was meant to be. He took another mouthful and chewed.

"She's said some decent things about us, right enough."

❧

Meredith straightened her hat. She stood outside the Browns' home. Jonah knocked. A light-haired woman in a dark blouse and skirt cracked the door. "Yes?"

Mrs. Cooper stepped forward, "May we come in?"

The woman's eyes warily rested on Meredith. The door creaked open. They followed Mrs. Brown to a couch and two chairs. After they were seated, the woman cast an anxious glance at Mrs. Cooper. "Is there a problem?"

"We hoped you could help us solve one."

The woman folded her hands in her lap.

"Is your son at home?" Amelia asked.

"No. He's working with his pa. I don't understand."

Jonah leaned forward, his elbows propped on his knees. "Your son has been a message courier for someone who has been sending offensive letters to Miss Mears. We are trying to find out who the writer is."

The woman's hand went to her breast. "My son has delivered these?"

"Yes. No fault lies at his door, but it's important that we find out whose behind this mischief and get it stopped."

"But, of course. I won't see him until tonight." She stood up and began to pace. "But rest assured, I shall find out. I'll send word as soon as I do."

"Thank you, ma'am," Jonah said.

"I'm sorry to have troubled you, Mrs. Brown," Mrs. Cooper said. "Please, don't worry about this. Like we said, it's not the boy's fault. But I knew you would want to help."

"I do," Mrs. Brown nodded vigorously.

Mrs. Cooper rose, and the others followed suit. "We'll run along, then, and wait to hear from you."

❧

Saturday evening, Mr. Brown and his son brought the news. The father cleared his lean throat and straightened his very tall frame. "We came to tell you that we know where the letters came from. They were from Frederick Ralston." He nudged his boy. "Right, son?"

Meredith flinched.

The boy nodded and kept his eyes to the floor. The father

placed his arm on his son's shoulder and gave it a squeeze.

"My boy didn't mean you no harm, Miss Mears."

"I understand. Thank you for telling me."

The boy looked up. "He made me promise not to tell who they was from."

"Don't worry," Mr. Brown said to his son. "After I speak with him, he won't harm you none."

"We do appreciate your coming here. May I get you both something to eat, to drink?" Mrs. Cooper asked.

"No. Thank you. His ma's rather anxious about this whole thing. We'll run along now. Sorry for our part in this."

Meredith smiled kindly at the lad and nodded.

When they had gone, Meredith eased into a chair. "I don't understand why that man is so hateful." Jonah handed Meredith his handkerchief. "There was plenty of room for both of us, but I won't write another article for that paper."

"We'll speak with him and the editor," Jonah said. "I'll go with you on Monday."

Meredith nodded, and there was a knock at the door. "That must be Mr. Talbot."

"I'll go answer it, dear," Amelia said.

"No. I want to get it."

"I'm off to my room," Jonah said.

"And I'll be in the kitchen if you need me," Amelia called on her way out.

Meredith dabbed her eyes with the handkerchief and made her way to the door. "Come in."

Thatcher followed Meredith wordlessly to the parlor and took the chair that was next to hers. "I've come at a bad time, haven't I?"

"Yes. But I was expecting you."

"Do you want to talk about it?"

She looked up at him from beneath dark wet lashes.

"Is it about the article?" He leaned forward and touched her arm. "That is entirely my fault. How can I ever say how sorry I am that I burst into the newspaper office and said all of those horrible things? I'm so sorry. Can you forgive me?"

"I just found out it was him."

Thatcher gave her an odd look. "Who else could it be?"

"No." She shook her head. "I mean he wrote those horrible letters I've been getting. They're threatening and ugly."

Thatcher withdrew his hand. "He wrote threatening letters to you?"

She twisted the handkerchief in her lap. "The boy who delivered them finally confessed that it was Frederick Ralston. He's done everything in his power to turn this town against me. It's time that I go. There's no need to wait another month."

"Please. Don't make any rash decisions."

"It's best."

"But what about us?"

Meredith was too overwrought to think clearly. "Us? You carry that wretched picture of your wife in your pocket and talk about us? What kind of man are you?"

"Are you still worrying about that picture? I told you she's nothing to me."

" 'To my husband, with all my love, Colleen,' " Meredith recited.

Thatcher's face paled. "Have you been mulling this over all this time? She's not my wife. I had no idea that you still thought such a thing."

"She's really not your wife?"

"Of course not. She's my best friend's wife. But she left him. He's the fellow I introduced you to the day I saw you trying on the hat."

Meredith mentally backtracked to that day. "Go on."

"His wife left him because he treated her badly. Now he's sorry, and he's trying to locate her. He passed through town and gave me this photograph in hopes that I might run across someone who had some information about her. I've been so busy at the camp and thinking about you that I haven't given it much thought. I thought you were jealous, that's all. I didn't think it would hurt anything."

The strain of the past several days weighed heavily on Meredith, and in a moment of sudden anger, with little regard to possible consequences, she jumped to her feet and shook her handkerchief at him.

"You fool! You had the audacity to barge into that newsroom and accuse me of all kinds of things because I didn't properly introduce my stepbrother to you, and yet you deliberately misled me to think you had an attachment or a wife. All this time I have thought. . .I have had it with you and this town!"

The word fool brought Thatcher to his feet. "Then I shall accommodate you, ma'am." With his stubborn reply, he picked up his hat and strode furiously toward the door to leave and lick his wounds. But first, he turned and smirked.

"Storm. The name suits you perfectly!"

Then he was gone.

His words hit her like a slap in the face. At last, she had driven him away. When she heard the door slam, she ran from the room and to the stairway. Partway up the steps, her weak ankle turned, and she collapsed on the staircase. Her hands flew out and grasped at the steps. The whole commotion brought Amelia from the kitchen and Jonah from his room.

She lay sprawled on the steps.

"Storm!"

twenty-five

Jonah helped Meredith to her feet. "Are you hurt?"

"Yes, but it doesn't matter," she whimpered.

With all of Meredith's weight shifted onto himself, Jonah asked, "Is it your ankle again?"

"He hates me. Everyone hates me."

"Oh, no, that's not true," Amelia said. "We love you."

"He doesn't! I've made such a mess of my life."

"Of course you haven't, Storm," Jonah said, easing her up into his arms and heading toward her room. "You've just had too much excitement for one evening."

"It'll all look better in the morning," Amelia said. "But let's take a look at that ankle. Perhaps we'll need the doctor."

Meredith groaned and lay back on her bed. "And how did he know my name?"

&

They did not call the doctor, for the sprain was not bad, but Meredith didn't go to church the following day. Instead, she sought the seclusion of her room and lay abed. She felt like packing up and going back to New York, but there was still the business of her unfinished story.

She considered her father, waiting to make amends, considered Asa, who trusted her to deliver. In the end, she opted to stick it out, square things with Ralston, and forget about Thatcher. It was just as well to end it this way.

That afternoon, Mrs. Bloomfield called on Meredith.

"At church today I heard about your fall. I'm so sorry you're not feeling well. Perhaps these will cheer you up."

The bouquet that Mrs. Bloomfield placed in one of Amelia's vases resembled Thatcher's droopy ones.

"Thank you," Meredith murmured.

140

"Oh, dear. You are blue today, aren't you?" Her friend seated herself on a nearby chair. "Is it more than just the ankle?"

Meredith gave a dismal nod and gazed off into space.

"Is it Thatcher again? What has he done this time?"

"It's me. I railed at him. He hates me now."

"I'm sure he doesn't. Perhaps his feelings are just hurt or something."

"I don't think there's much hope left between us. It's better this way. But it's so hard."

"I understand. We won't talk about it anymore, then."

"Perhaps it's time for me to return to New York City."

"Oh, but you can't go now. You must at least stay until after Pride Day."

"Did you say Pride Day?"

Beatrice nodded enthusiastically.

Meredith moaned, "I have enough trouble with pride, and you celebrate it?"

Mrs. Bloomfield tilted her head. "It's the day we clean up the town. We replace floors and sidewalks that the loggers tear up. Everyone chips in, and we clean up the whole town."

"That is the most amazing thing I've ever heard. You're absolutely right. I wouldn't want to miss a thing like that. It'll make a wonderful story."

❧

Monday morning, things looked clearer to Meredith. Her ankle felt tender but strong enough to carry her weight. Jonah insisted that they take care of things at the newspaper office so Meredith could get her life back in order. He brought a wagon around from the stables.

The bell announced their arrival, and Meredith limped into the newsroom with a great deal of grace.

"I've come to settle some matters." She coveted the closest chair to her. "May I sit?"

The editor-in-chief motioned toward the chair with a nod and glanced at Jonah, who hovered over Meredith. "Is there a problem?"

Meredith pulled several wrinkled pieces of paper from her portfolio and thrust them in the air. "These are threatening letters written to me. The boy who delivered them said that they came from you." Her eyes settled on Mr. Ralston.

His face turned hateful. "Can't take the truth, Miss Mears?"

"Let me see those." The editor snapped the letters off the floor and leafed through them. When he was finished, he turned a condemning gaze on his male reporter. "This is the lowest thing I have ever seen. You're fired."

"No!" Meredith's hand shot up in the air. "He stays. I quit. I'm leaving soon anyway."

She turned toward Ralston. "But I want to set the record straight. I was never after your job. This has only been a temporary assignment. You knew that from the start. The logging camp was an assignment for *McClure's* magazine. I don't know why you hate me so, but I didn't come to get you fired. I just came to tell you that I know you wrote those letters. You can quit writing them. You can have your job, and you'll get your way soon enough. I'm leaving in September."

She rose from her chair and faced the editor. "I'm through here, but I thank you for the work you've given me."

"Wait a minute," the editor said. "I'm not finished. Ralston, you're still fired. That was the most ungentlemanly thing to do. I don't need your kind representing this paper."

The pale reporter glared at Meredith and at the editor. "I don't need this cheap operation. And I surely don't need a woman bossing me around. I quit." He threw a few things together and started to leave; at the door he turned back, a wicked smirk on his face. "But you're still a tramp and a liar, Miss Uppity."

Jonah lunged toward the door.

"Jonah. Let it be," Meredith said.

The reporter gave the photographer a parting hateful look and fled.

Jonah chased after him and returned within moments. "He's gone."

Meredith slumped back into the chair and dipped her head in her hands.

"I'm ashamed for the trouble he's caused you, ma'am. I'll get you something to drink. You look pale." The editor left them to fetch the drink.

Jonah knelt beside Meredith's chair and grinned up at her. "You were beautiful."

She smiled. "So were you."

The editor returned with a drink of water, and Meredith accepted it gratefully. He apologized again and said, "The job is yours, you know. On behalf of this town, we'd love for you to stay."

She shook her head. "I don't think so."

"No." The editor's hand shot up. "Don't answer me today. You're too distressed. Take your time and think about it."

❧

Meredith slept on it and the next day returned to the editor's office.

"I appreciate your offer. I feel terrible to have cost you a valuable reporter, especially since I'm only staying until September. But in the meantime, I'd be glad to fill in if I can also work on my articles for *McClure's*."

"The facilities are at your disposal."

"I won't be going to the logging camp anymore," Meredith said. "But I'll be doing some research by mail and continuing the story. I plan to stop at a few camps on the trip home."

"Sounds good to me."

"So what's my first assignment?"

"I thought we should do a blurb, 'Reporter leaves town.' Nothing too informative, unless it's too painful."

"I'll get right on it, boss."

❧

Meredith worked hard at the newspaper. She did not ride back to the logging camp and did not run into Mr. Talbot, so things settled down for her in town.

twenty-six

Two Saturdays passed from the time that Thatcher walked out of Meredith's life. She had not seen him since. Each Saturday a tiny hope rose within her that maybe he would show up on her doorstep. But it never happened. It was Saturday again, and Meredith felt restless. She decided Jonah's studio would provide a proper diversion.

It was raining, so she donned a jacket, but Amelia intercepted her by the door. "And where do you think you're going in this rain?"

"Just to the studio to chat with Jonah. Want to come?"

"Oh. Well. . ." Amelia gazed longingly toward the studio, but her practical disposition won out in the end. "No. One foolish woman in this household is enough. You'll need someone to nurse you again."

Meredith giggled. "You're probably right. But it's not like I'm going far."

"But it's pouring."

"And I'll hurry," Meredith said, before bursting outside.

"Watch your ankle!" Amelia shouted after her.

Meredith chuckled as she ran, but wisely kept her eyes downcast and watched her step, then danced up and down in the rain, waiting for Jonah to answer her knock.

"Come in," he yelled.

She pushed open the door, and a gust of wind blew her in.

"Storm?" He could not stop his particular task without harming his photographs, but his eyes flashed concern. "What are you doing out in the rain?"

"Visiting you."

He caught her playful mood. "I can see that. You're dripping all over my floor."

"So what are you working on?"

"Photographs of the dock. The ocean is a wonderful backdrop."

"Mm-hmm. That schooner looks majestic sitting on top of that wave."

"Unique, isn't it?"

"So, Jonah." She leisurely milled about the studio, fingering different things and looking at his finished works. "You've done a wonderful job with this studio. But where are you going to live after I leave?"

"Pardon?" His head bobbed up and down as he dipped paper in and out of a solution.

"It wouldn't look proper for you to live here alone with Amelia."

He frowned. "I've given it some thought, but haven't come up with a solution yet."

"I have one," she ventured. "Why don't you marry her?"

The paper slipped from his hands and down into the pan of solution. "Now look what you've gone and done."

She moved closer and leaned over his shoulder as he removed it. "Is it ruined?"

"Fortunately for you, it's not."

"So?"

"I guess that would be one possible solution."

"Have you considered it?"

"I have."

She giggled. "And?"

He smiled. "I rather like the idea."

"You sly old fox, you." She sidled up to him.

"Watch it. Stay back."

"Well?" she pressed.

"A few weeks does not give a man enough time to court, propose, and marry, does it now?"

She laughed with delight and grabbed his arm. "Congratulations, old man."

"Watch it now, Storm. Be careful there."

"Maybe she'd let you stay at the mill. But you'd better start making your intentions known if you expect such a favor."

His hands stopped midair, and his eyes lit with hope. "That's a great idea. There's plenty of room there. Surely there would be someplace. . .and Amelia does have the connections." He grinned appreciatively at her. "Thanks, Storm."

"You're welcome." She hugged his stiff body, for he held his soupy hands out away from her. "I just want you to be happy."

"I am. I love it here."

"Good. Well, I'd better get back to the house. Talking with you has given me the lift I needed."

She ran back to the house, and Amelia appeared almost as soon as the door opened. "See how wet you got! What's a body to do?" she scolded.

Meredith gave her a sly smile. "Let's sit by the fire, shall we? So I can dry off."

❦

The next day, a steady rain continued. Jonah dressed in a slicker and went to the stables around the corner. He returned with Amelia's horse and carriage. Bundled up in summer coats, Meredith and Amelia scurried into the protection of the carriage. All the way to church, Amelia chatted on and on about how poor Jonah would be drenched.

"He'll be fine. He's dressed appropriately. Anyway, it makes him feel chivalrous to do this for us," Meredith said.

"You think so?"

"I know Jonah. I'm sure of it."

With that, Amelia seemed appeased.

❦

At the small church, they scurried inside, allowing Jonah to take care of the horses and carriage. Spirits weren't gloomy in spite of the weather; folks smiled and greeted each other as normal. When Meredith pulled her hooded cape back away from her face, she saw something that gave her a start. Across the entryway stood a dripping but handsome Thatcher Talbot.

❧

Thatcher saw Meredith enter. Her rosy cheeks and sparkling eyes almost took his breath away. Now he knew he had been a fool to come. He should have waited until she had gone back to New York. God would have understood. When her hands faltered and her gaze rested upon him, he looked away and engaged the nearest person in a conversation about the weather.

❧

Meredith's cheeks burned at Thatcher's snub. She tried to look away, to enter into the conversation of the nearby circle of women. Her smile was weak, and her hands felt icy. She couldn't tell how much time passed until they all shuffled into the sanctuary, and she tried to ignore Thatcher, but nevertheless, she noticed him sitting a few pews back on the opposite side.

Good. Out of sight. Now if I can only keep the back of my neck from turning red.

The sermon was on forgiveness and was most compelling. Meredith lost herself in the Word of God. The preacher explained no sin was too large to forgive. She would have to think about that. He explained that a person is saved by grace and since one sin is as bad as another, all can be forgiven by God and should be forgiven by man.

All too soon for Meredith, the service ended. Just as she knew they would, her rebellious eyes sought out Thatcher Talbot. It almost looked as though he were purposely waiting for her. Or was he waiting for the rain to slow? Her heart gave a foolish flutter, and before she could do a thing about it, her legs propelled her forward, down the center aisle.

Please someone stop me. Oh, where is Beatrice Bloomfield when I need her?

"Hello, Meredith."

If he was so bold as to use her first name after what had passed between them, then she would be just as brave.

"Hello, Thatcher."

He looked toward the window. "Quite the cloudburst."

Thatcher looked so forlorn, so vulnerable. Meredith heard herself say, "Given the preacher's sermon on forgiveness, I feel the fool standing here talking to you."

He looked at his boots then up again. "Meredith. . ."

"I'm sorry for getting so angry," she said.

"Me, too."

There was a lengthy silence, and then she said, "Something's been plaguing me since our last meeting."

He arched his brows, leaned forward, and whispered, "Knowing us and our past experiences, I'm not sure this is a safe place to start another serious discussion."

Her hand shot out and touched his arm briefly, and he quieted.

"Ask," he said.

Her hand slipped back down to her side. She leaned close and whispered, "How did you know my name?"

"That bothered you, did it?"

She gave him an earnest nod. "It hurt, but I deserved it."

"The day your horse appeared in camp without you, Jonah came riding up to the group of men gathered there. The bull asked him if he knew where you were. Jonah said, *You mean Storm?* No one else caught it, but I'd always wondered what that middle initial stood for. The instant he said it, I knew."

"I should have known. He calls me that all the time. It's what I go by back home. But I told him I didn't want people here to know. You might as well stamp volatile across my face in big red letters."

Thatcher laughed. It grew quiet between them again for a while, and then he turned pensive. "I had to think of my father during the preacher's sermon."

"Me, too." She waited and when he didn't say anything more, she added, "When Charles was here," she gave him a tentative glance, "he told me that my father is sorry for our argument. He actually sent Charles to see how I fared." She shook her head. "It's almost more than I can hope that things might improve with Father."

He touched her arm. "Why, that's wonderful news. You must believe."

"I've been praying about it."

"Then it must be God at work."

"What about you? Will you ever return to your father to try and make amends?"

"You don't know my father. But I have thought about it. I know I will someday. I just want the time to be right."

"You're praying about it then?"

"Yes, I am."

Amelia interrupted them. "Jonah has our carriage. Are you ready, Meredith?"

"Yes. I'll be right there."

Meredith turned back to Thatcher. "I'm glad we had this talk."

"I wish I could see you home. But all I have is a horse."

"I'm leaving for New York very soon. It's probably just as well."

Thatcher watched her walk away, then hurry through the rain and climb into Mrs. Cooper's carriage. He watched it slosh away, disappointed Meredith hadn't invited him over for the afternoon.

twenty-seven

Thatcher ate his lunch at a table in the hotel's dining room and gazed out the window. The street was deserted except for an occasional carriage or intrepid horseback rider. He didn't relish riding back to camp in the rain; the ride from the church to the hotel had been bad enough.

"We have berry pie for dessert."

Thatcher looked away from the steamy window just long enough to answer the waitress.

"Pie sounds good."

The pie was just an excuse to put off the inevitable decision. Would he go see Meredith? At the church, she had said it was better if they didn't pursue their relationship. *But,* he wondered, *did she really mean it?*

The waitress returned with his pie just as an unexpected patch of sun broke through the sky, and by the time he had eaten the last bite, the rain had ceased entirely. He paid for his meal and strode outside.

The air was rain scented with musty forest and wet soil odors. The eastern sky shone hopefully bright; he could probably make it to camp. To the west, the Cooper house lay beyond his vision, the sky dark and threatening.

He would return to camp.

è

The whole next week, Meredith wavered between wishing she had invited Thatcher over on Sunday to feeling confident that she had been right to discourage him.

Regardless, she kept busy. She sent Jonah to the logging camp with the conservation suggestions she had promised the bull and hand-delivered the same information to the mill. Her correspondence research was going well, her work at the newspaper, time consuming. The most interesting business at hand was also the talk of the town, Pride Day.

Finally, Saturday, the long-awaited and highly praised Pride Day arrived. The mill prepared and donated wagonloads of special materials for repairs. The mill owner drafted a blueprint of the areas needing repair and posted it on a sign in front of the general store on Main Street.

Main Street, the hub of activity, was one of the major areas that needed work. Jonah set up a tripod for his camera on the far side of the street. The mahogany camera was shined to a high gloss, and its brass hardware twinkled in the sunlight.

Meredith positioned her station of refreshments nearby. She kept the water barrel full and food tables of sandwiches and cookies ready for the working men. Meredith purposely wore a large-pocketed apron to stash writing supplies so she could jot down notes throughout the day.

Men ripped up damaged sidewalk boards with wicked-looking crowbars and threw them into the streets, where others picked them up and tossed them onto a wagon. When the wagon was full, it was taken to the mill. Nails would later be removed so the scraps could be given out as free firewood. The rest would go in the big stoves at the mill.

Meredith marveled and wrote notes about the small amount of waste. Pride Day would make a fitting conclusion to Meredith's articles, using Buckman's Pride and Bucker's Stand to demonstrate good conservation methods to the entire West Coast.

"Doing two jobs at once, I see."

"Good morning, Beatrice. One keeps my mind busy and the other my hands."

"There's plenty today for both. I love this day and the way the town pulls together." The banker's wife wore an old dark skirt and white blouse. She balanced several pans of freshly baked cookies.

"Are you here to help serve?"

"Oh, no. I'm washing windows."

"You don't say? Well, that's a noble thing to do."

"All I know, I've done it every year since I've lived here, and every year I'm so weary by the end of the day that I vow I'll never do it again. But, here I am."

Meredith giggled. "Amelia Cooper says that every year she gets a kink in her neck from knocking cobwebs out of the rafters. I feel guilty doing such an easy job."

"Toting those water buckets isn't easy. Wait till the end of the day. That's when you can tell how hard you've worked."

Meredith thought about the saddle blisters and other hardships she had endured on this assignment. She doubted if anyone understood how hard she worked. The satisfaction that came with a job well done was pay enough. She bade Beatrice good-bye and turned her attention to the various other activities taking place around her.

"Hello," a shy voice said.

Meredith looked up. It was the Swedish woman from the lumber camp. "Well, hello."

"It's all so exciting, isn't it? Can you use some help?"

"Yes, it is exciting, and I would love some help."

The young blond moved behind the table. Then the two women fell into a companionable time of conversing and working together.

ᶻ

Meredith saw Thatcher. She had secretly been watching for him all morning. Thatcher's sleeves were rolled up, and his lower arms bulged with muscles acquired from his weeks at the logging camp. He hoisted several pieces of lumber up over his shoulder. She watched him shoulder his load with seeming ease, every muscle a fluid motion. He dropped the load onto another stack of lumber and turned. Their eyes met, and Thatcher gave her a large smile.

He knew that whole time that I was watching him, Meredith thought with shame. She gave him a small nod, then fussed at the table. *What an irritating man.* She rearranged and tidied things, trying to work with a semblance of normalcy.

She knew that every hardworking man eventually helped himself from the water and food at her table. Still, when Thatcher appeared it felt awkward, and her hand shook uncontrollably. She placed it behind her back. The Swedish woman dipped out his drink. She and Thatcher were acquainted from the camp.

"Saw you working over here," Thatcher said to Meredith, his eyes suspiciously merry.

"I saw you working over there," Meredith returned. "Trying not to miss a thing. It's all going to make a great story, what the loggers are doing for the town." He dipped out his second glass of water himself. "It's not just the loggers, everyone pitches in, even pretty reporters."

"Help yourself to some sandwiches and cookies," the Swedish woman interrupted, then discreetly found something with which to occupy herself.

He studied her a moment. "Meredith, I'm dining at my friends, the Bloomfields. May I call on you afterwards?"

"I don't know. I. . ."

"Please, Meredith." His eyes were dark, soulful, imploring her to yield. Finally, she nodded.

With a newfound boldness, he said, "I shall be able to get twice as much done, now, with such a reward awaiting me at the end of the day."

When he had left, she said to herself, *And I shall get nothing done if I keep watching you.*

"I think he has his eyes on you," Meredith's Swedish friend said. Meredith spun around. She gave a weak wave. "Him?"

"Ya, him."

Meredith just shrugged, relieved when a group of loggers approached their table. This time, she leaned forward to be the one to help.

twenty-eight

The sterling silver brush made long, even strokes through Meredith's clean brown hair. She wanted to look her best for Thatcher. Regardless, if they were meant to be together or not, she wanted to make this evening special, one they could always remember. She would allow him to make his move, if he intended to make one.

There was such little time left until she returned to New York. She knew she loved him. It was true that she did not want to make the necessary sacrifices of becoming a logger's wife, but maybe it was not his intention to be a logger the rest of his life. She only hoped that he had some wonderful plan to sweep her off her feet.

Her fingers nimbly went to work arranging her hair in a long style, swept up from the face, but hanging loose in the back. She slipped into her gown and shoes and went to the window that overlooked Amelia's backyard. There was a light on in Jonah's studio.

Jonah had taken several photographs of Pride Day that would complement her story. It would be a good one, she knew. Even if she never stepped foot inside a camp that needed to hear about conservation or saw with her own eyes the devastation that she had read about, her stories would make a difference. It would be hard to leave this place. The people had grown dear to her.

Especially Thatcher. She had tried her hardest to keep him from slipping into her heart, but looking back, she believed he had done so that very first time she had laid eyes on him on the train from Chicago. She drew away from the window and started toward her bedroom door.

What lay in store for her hopeful heart tonight? Would

Thatcher make the declarations she wanted to hear?

ஜ

Meanwhile, Thatcher had just finished helping Beatrice with the dishes. His spirits were high. His friends had entertained him hospitably with simple fare, since everyone felt fatigued from the day's hard work.

Thatcher's mind was on Meredith. There was such little time to profess his love and win hers before she went back to the elegance of New York City.

He unrolled his shirtsleeves. "Beatrice, this has been a most enjoyable time. The meal was delicious."

"You've already thanked me a dozen times, Thatcher," she said.

"Don't spoil her. I have to live with her," Herbert said.

"I have a confession to make," Thatcher said.

"So that's it. Well, have a seat and tell all," Beatrice said.

Thatcher seated himself and looked sheepishly from his hostess to his host, although he knew they would understand when he told them of his plans to call on Meredith.

"I. . ." He stopped. Someone had knocked at the door.

"Excuse me," Herbert said.

Beatrice shrugged, and she and Thatcher both eyed the hall, waiting to find out who the caller was.

"William Boon! What a surprise. Do come in."

Thatcher jerked. William was back? In moments, the two men entered the room. It was Thatcher's old friend from Chicago. They greeted each other all around.

"What timing! To find you here as well, Thatcher. For I haven't much time. In fact, I thought I might not see you at all. I'm moving on tomorrow."

"What's the rush?" Thatcher asked.

"Father's ill."

William's face looked worried, deeply lined. Thatcher thought he looked travel worn, not the city gentleman he had seen only weeks earlier.

"You know how long it takes for word to reach you when

you're always on the move. I've no time to waste. And then there's the family business. Mother will need my help."

"Any word of Colleen?" Thatcher asked.

"That's the worst of it." Thatcher's friend looked broken, as if he might weep at any moment, but he continued in a weary voice. "I was so close. I found out that she is alone and pregnant with our child."

"Are you sure you should turn back?"

"I don't know if I'm doing the right thing or not. But even if I found her, she might not return with me. Now that I know where she is, I'll hire someone to go after her. I feel I must return to Father first."

Thatcher wanted to insist, *But she's with child, your child.* But it wouldn't do any good to argue with a decision already made. He would have to support his friend and pray for God to protect Colleen and their unborn child.

Beatrice served leftover cookies from Meredith's food table. "You must be starved," she said to William.

Thatcher suddenly realized how much time had passed and that he was supposed to be calling upon Meredith. A sinking feeling pulled him. He knew it was too late to call now. The time had slipped away. His friend needed him. He tried to push the consequences of what this would do to his relationship with Meredith out of his mind as he politely took the offered cookies.

❧

At the Cooper residence, Meredith waited patiently at first, chatting with Amelia. As time passed, however, and her friend's gaze became more sympathetic, Meredith paced the room.

Finally, she said, "He isn't coming. I suppose it's just as well."

"I'm sure he has a good explanation."

"I suppose he just forgot."

"No, Mr. Talbot would never forget. Don't think the worst, my dear. Trust that something came up. You'll probably get the whole explanation tomorrow."

"Tomorrow?"

Meredith could not remember a time she had ever gotten stood up by a gentleman, except her father, of course. She hadn't had that many callers because her father had wanted to keep her at home to care for the house. When she went to work at the magazine and found her own place to live, there had been some men interested in her, and they had never left her waiting in the lurch.

"I think I'll go to bed now. It's been an exhausting day."

ಜಿ

The next day, Meredith opened her eyes with dread. Church. Thatcher might be there. She didn't want to listen to his excuses or see his infuriating smirk. If she stayed at home, however, he would think she was pining over him. That wouldn't do. Reluctantly, she dragged herself out of the security of her bed and began to dress.

The moment Meredith entered the church house, Thatcher and Beatrice Bloomfield bore down upon her. *So he brings a buffer.* Meredith's face twitched unnaturally as the pair drew closer.

"My dear, Meredith," Beatrice said, extending her hand, "I have come to plead for Thatcher." Her other hand was set securely in the crook of his arm. "Last night an old friend dropped in just as he was preparing to call upon you. Thatcher was in the very act of making his apologies, of getting ready to leave. Our visitor from Chicago was only going to be in town that night, and he was so beset with personal problems. The time slipped away."

Meredith felt amused. Thatcher was turning red. "I see," she said.

Beatrice released her grip on Thatcher's arm and turned to him. "Forgive me, Thatcher, for interfering so," she said then turned back to Meredith. "I only wanted to help. Please, hear him out. He speaks the truth. There was nothing we could do."

Meredith watched Beatrice depart.

Thatcher started where Mrs. Bloomfield left off. "His arrival was so abrupt, so unexpected that by the time I could have sent you word, it was too late. I'm so sorry. I had truly looked forward to seeing you all day yesterday. You can't imagine how much it meant to me."

He looked sincere.

"Where is your friend now?" Meredith gazed about the room for this invisible scapegoat.

"He had to leave early this morning. His father is ill, perhaps dying. He has many troubles. You do believe me, don't you?"

"Of course," she said. To her irritation, her face twitched again.

He leaned close. "Beatrice felt so bad that she made us a picnic lunch. Please, say you'll share it with me."

"I don't know. I'll have to think about it. I'm going to find a seat now."

Meredith could feel Thatcher's pleading eyes burn her back as she walked away.

The sermon seemed long and, as always, convicting. As Meredith turned her eyes upon God and felt His grace and forgiveness anew, she realized that she must forgive Thatcher one more time and allow him the opportunity to speak his mind.

The service was barely over when Thatcher appeared at her side. "Will you come with me?"

"Yes. For if I don't, I know that I'll receive Mrs. Bloomfield's wrath."

"I'll accept any reason you give me. I want to be with you."

Meredith felt her walls tumbling down again as she allowed Thatcher to make the final arrangements and whisk her away in the banker's carriage. They stopped by the river.

"This place is wonderful. How did you find it?"

"The Bloomfields told me about it."

"Seems they're matchmaking."

Thatcher chuckled. "You should know by now that I need all the help I can get." He artfully arranged their blanket and food, talking as he worked. "I've done nothing but bumble our relationship from the start."

Meredith settled in beside him, setting her gaze on the river, wishing he could convince her of his loyalty. They enjoyed the picnic, and Thatcher continued to woo her throughout, making it one of the happiest moments of her life.

"Thank you for bringing me here," she said softly.

"I feel so helpless," he said.

"Why?"

"I care so much about you, and I feel you slipping away. Our time is so short. I don't have the finesse to do this right. Can you forgive me for all my clumsiness?" He reached out a finger and traced her cheek, her chin.

She leaned into his touch. "It's not been all your fault. We have wasted time, haven't we?"

"Oh yes," he said.

She wanted to ask him, *What now?*

His soft suede eyes drew close, and he tipped her chin. She felt his sweet breath before his lips tenderly kissed her. And then she knew that she could never go on in life without him. Her hand went up to touch his face. When they parted, he searched her face and murmured those words she longed to hear.

"I love you, Storm."

twenty-nine

Meredith floated through breakfast and later floated over the town's new boardwalks. She was in love with the most wonderful man in the world. She had no idea love could be so wonderful. They had not made any plans, but Thatcher prom-ised to call midweek. He said he would follow her to the East Coast if that's what it took to prove his love sincere.

She stopped humming long enough to open the door to the general store, where the post office was located. The owner knew her quite well by now. "Good morning, to you," he said. As he nodded, his glasses worked forward on his nose, and a quick swipe of his hands set them back in place.

"Anything for me?"

"You must be expecting something good. You sure look happy this morning." He handed her an envelope, and the door swung open again.

"Thank you," she said, leaving him to help the next person. As she moved back outside and her boots hit the taut wooden sidewalk, she was reminded of the recent repairs and let her eyes fall across the walkway.

A shadow fell across her path. The sun had moved behind a cloud. She glanced up. *Hope it doesn't rain. Nothing could ruin this day.* And she even had a letter from Asa.

She slit it open with her fingernail and pulled it out to read as she made her way to the newspaper office. She blinked. Her steps faltered. Unconsciously, she reached out for a nearby post. She leaned her shoulder into it and blinked back tears as she let each word sink into her mind.

Storm,

I've received news on Mr. Talbot. Sorry it is so slow in coming. But you were right, he does have a reward out on him, only not by the law. The reward, strangely enough, is being offered by his own father. Seems he left his father short-handed in the business and ran out on some woman besides. His father is hoping to find his whereabouts and bring him home to face up to his responsibilities. So I guess it's a family scandal of some sort. Hope that helps. Looking forward to seeing you again. Keep up the excellent work.

Asa

Family scandal, ran out on a woman.

Instantly, the photograph came to Meredith's mind. He had told her about his father, but what if he weren't telling the entire story, but only the parts he wanted to tell. What if he had run out on a wife? What other explanation was there if his own father was searching for him? It was not the woman who had run off, it was Thatcher. And, it was not his friend's problem, it was Thatcher's. Of course, this explained everything.

Why had he turned against his own wife? Did he truly love Meredith? It mattered not. He was married. He had many responsibilities.

ð

Somehow, Meredith floundered through the remainder of the day. And the next day, with a desperate resolve, she threw herself into her work to wrap up all loose ends. If only Charles would arrive early. She wanted to leave today, now. But it was impossible.

Thatcher would call on her midweek. He would break her heart again. In the days that followed, she nursed her hurts and rehearsed what she would say to Thatcher.

ð

Midweek finally rolled around. Meredith was working in the newsroom. Her editor walked into the room with an intense expression on his face.

"Something wrong?" she asked.

"I figured out what Ralston had against you," Charlie said.

Meredith turned full around in her chair. "Oh?"

"Seems he had a bad record with his past employers." Charlie gave a sheepish look. "When he arrived, I was so hard up for help that I didn't check his references. I was curious after he left and made some inquiries."

"I don't understand."

"He's been fired before, and I think he was just plain worried about keeping his job."

Meredith shook her head. "I feel sorry for him."

"I don't. You ready to quit for the day? I've got a banking errand here for you, if you are."

"Sure."

Meredith left the newsroom, glad to be able to put the mystery of Ralston behind her, but troubled over the impending situation with Thatcher. She stopped in at the bank to make the deposit for her employer, her mind mulling over her problem.

"You look preoccupied," Herbert Bloomfield said. "Working on a problem?"

"That's what Jonah always says to me. I must be a mirror."

"Most women are. Speaking of," his head motioned in the direction of his home, "the wife has some news she wants to share with you. I know that she would love it if you stopped in."

Meredith needed to stay busy. She certainly wouldn't need any time to primp tonight. She wasn't even going to change her clothes. And if Thatcher had to wait on her, all the better.

"I'll stop in now. Thank you."

She made her way past the few buildings down to the end of the street and turned the corner where the Bloomfields lived, ill prepared for what she saw: Thatcher's horse. Should she retreat? She felt adrenaline pulse through her veins; her anger surfaced.

She would get this over with, once and for all. She marched

forward with purposeful steps and tapped on the door. Beatrice greeted her with a hug.

"I wanted to see you. Sit down. I have something special to tell you."

She gripped the back of the chair instead. "Is Thatcher here?"

"Well, yes."

"In there?" She nodded toward the back parlor.

"Yes, but. . ."

"I'll just be a moment, if you don't mind." Meredith tossed her head and started toward the sitting room.

Beatrice followed close behind.

What Meredith saw caused her to halt. A wave of nausea swept over her. Thatcher and the woman of the photograph were wrapped in each other's arms. Her mouth flew open to spew out hateful accusations, and then she remembered that this was Thatcher's wife. She snapped her mouth closed and turned, running headlong into Beatrice.

Thatcher looked up and released Colleen, as if she were live coals. Instantly, he moved toward Meredith.

"Storm."

"Stay away from me!"

His arms extended toward her.

"And keep those filthy hands to yourself."

"Meredith, wait. It isn't what it seems."

"It seems," she spat, "that you're going to be a daddy. Congratulations."

With that she pushed past Beatrice and fled out the door. She heard him call out her name again. "She's my friend's wife. Listen to me."

Meredith kept walking.

"I have to leave for a while. I'm taking her to San Francisco. But I'll be back for you. I'll find you if I have to search New York City every day for the rest of my life."

"Let her go," Beatrice said. "Meredith won't listen now. She's too angry. Maybe I can explain later. Come back in, Thatcher."

Thatcher knew Beatrice was right and returned with reluctance. Colleen needed him. Meredith hated him.

≈

Meredith broke into a run and burst into the Cooper home in a flood of tears.

"Whatever's wrong?" Amelia asked.

"Leave me alone!" Meredith pushed past Amelia and ran up the steps to her room. The door slammed.

"What's wrong with her?" Amelia asked. "She's acted so strange all week."

Jonah frowned. "I would imagine it has something to do with Mr. Talbot. I knew the moment I laid eyes on him that he and Meredith would have a hard time of it. They fell for each other from the start."

"Lover's quarrel?"

"Probably." He made his way toward Amelia and laid his hand upon her shoulder. "Speaking of love. I think it's time we had a talk of our own."

Mrs. Cooper's eyes flew open, and Jonah led her toward the nearest chair.

"Amelia. I have a great admiration for you. Would you allow me to court you?"

The older woman swallowed then lowered her eyes. "I believe I would."

"I only hope we don't have as much trouble as that pair." His eyes looked toward the stairway.

"I don't expect we shall," she replied.

thirty

Meredith threw herself on her bed and cried out to God.

"Help me. O God, help me."

She continued her tantrum for a few minutes more, but as the supplication kept pouring from her lips, a peace flooded over her. Meredith recognized it as God's love. He loved her now, when she needed Him most.

"Forgive me, Lord," she prayed. "You are the one I've been searching for. It is You whom I need."

His love enveloped her, and it was as if new pages of Meredith's mind were turned, and all of this understanding floated off the pages and into her heart. Every part of her knew that she had been going about everything the wrong way, making all the decisions, pushing, pushing, pushing. She'd been trying to control her father, trying to make love happen or not happen.

"I've not kept my eyes on You, Jesus. Forgive me. Your peace and love are better than any earthly person's. You are all I need. Thank you for showing Yourself to me."

She would survive. Her God would never forsake her, though she turned back and forth to Him like an old toy. In an ongoing prayer of praise and confession, Meredith finally dropped off into an exhausted sleep.

When she awoke, God's name remained on her lips. "You are still here. Live in me. Then I can live," she prayed.

&

At noon, Meredith felt doubly blessed. Her brother arrived early. She threw herself into his arms with a wild abandonment. "I'm so glad you arrived early. I want to go."

"Do I have time to rest up?"

Her expression turned serious. "Of course. How much

time?" Then she recalled that the Prince of Peace resided in her, and she didn't need to push. "Take all the time you need. I'm just excited, is all."

"We'll leave in the morning."

Jonah pushed away from the table where they had been sharing a lunch. "I'd best be packing my things also."

Meredith realized what her leaving meant for Jonah. He would have to leave this house.

"But where will you go?"

He grinned at her. "The mill. Don't worry. Amelia and I have all the details worked out, don't we, dear?"

Amelia blushed, and Meredith covered her hand with her mouth. "You mean. . .?"

"Yes, dear," Amelia replied.

"I'm so happy for you," Meredith said.

"Seems as if you've come a long way since last night," Amelia said.

Meredith turned serious again. "I apologize for my rudeness. I'm going to be all right now. I'm letting God rule my life. All of it."

Meredith saw her friend's face soften and wondered what her brother thought of her declaration. But it didn't matter. A deep, abiding peace flowed through her. In fact, she was so full of God's love that the thought even went through her mind, *If all that has happened to me with Thatcher, with my father, happened only so that I could truly find God, then it was all worth it. And whatever lies ahead would all be worth it even if I only had this one day of God's love to experience. But I don't. I have a lifetime. God is so good.*

"I'd best go pack," she said.

"Let me know if you need help," Amelia called.

First Meredith arranged all of her writing in a neat stack and placed it in the bottom of one of her travelling bags. She took a look around to decide what would go in next when a light tap sounded on her bedroom door.

"Come in."

It was Mrs. Bloomfield. "Amelia just told me you're leaving."

Meredith pulled out the chair from her desk and offered, "Please, sit down."

As her friend sat, Meredith cleared a spot on the bed and sat also. "I wish to apologize for last night. I was rude and thoughtless."

The woman's hand sliced through the air. "Nonsense." She looked about the uprooted room. "I wish you didn't have to go and that I had your pluck and courage."

"Don't wish it. I've learned a better way." She rubbed her palms against her skirt. "I've given everything over to God, and I feel so much better." Then she waved her hand. "I'm through being a progressive woman. Now I'm. . ." She tilted her head, looking for the right word. "Just God's."

"I can see there's a new peace about you. You were so angry last night."

Meredith chose not to think about Thatcher and asked instead, "Your husband said you had some news, a surprise. What were you trying to tell me?"

Beatrice smiled deeply and even turned a little red. "We're going to have a baby."

The words hit Meredith with such impact that she flew to her feet and rushed to kneel before her friend. "I'm so happy for you. How wonderful."

"I'm so happy." Beatrice sighed. "But my happiness would be complete if only you and Thatcher could make amends."

Meredith rose, backed up a few steps. "How can you say that when you know that he's married?"

"Thatcher isn't married."

"He has you fooled, too. The woman that he was with. He carries her photograph. It is signed from his loving wife." She saw Beatrice's look of shock. "Perhaps you don't know. There's some sort of scandal with his family. His father has a reward out on him. He ran off on that woman. His wife."

"No, no." Beatrice shook her head. "I know all about it, but you've got it wrong. Thatcher is not married. That is his friend's wife. The one who ruined your plans the other night. Our friend was searching for her, but then his father got sick. When Colleen appeared and needed help, Thatcher agreed to help her get home. She's pregnant."

Meredith plopped back onto the bed. "I saw." The pieces fell into place. "You're sure?"

"Of course, I'm sure. Thatcher is the most upstanding man. Even all his father's money could not corrupt him after he became a Christian. When we heard what was happening in Chicago, we encouraged Thatcher to come to Buckman's Pride and visit us. The idea of working at the logging camp intrigued him from the moment we suggested it. You can trust Thatcher, Meredith."

She shook her head regretfully. "If he is all that, then he surely doesn't deserve me."

"Nonsense. He loves you."

Meredith remembered Thatcher's declaration of love. "It's too late. My brother's here. It's time to go."

"Please, don't leave with things like this."

"God is in control now. Thatcher knows where to find me if he wants to. I hate to leave you and all my friends, but I must go."

"I'll write to you."

"Come visit me."

"Perhaps I shall."

❧

That afternoon Meredith went by the newsroom to pick up her things and say farewell to the editor. She glanced sadly at the sign in his window. *Reporter wanted.* She stopped by the mill and left a letter at the post office for the bull at Bucker's Stand. This town would always hold a special place in her heart.

The following morning, she unashamedly let the tears flow as she hugged Amelia and Jonah good-bye. She gave them both her blessings, and then Meredith and her brother rode out of town.

❧

That evening, around a campfire, memories flooded Meredith. She remembered Silas, who had guided her and Jonah through these woods, and the campfires she had faced with them. But most of all, she remembered the night she was lost in the woods with Thatcher.

She had treated Thatcher shabbily from the start. He was an honest man, and she had probed into his painful personal life and harbored accusations against him from the start. He had loved her, and she had spurned him at every turn.

She let out a deep regretful sigh.

"Are you sure you want to leave?" Charles asked.

"It's only that I learned too late."

"Learned what too late?"

"To trust God. To trust the man I loved."

"I think it's time you told me the whole story. We've got all night. What's going on in your life, Storm?"

Meredith told her brother the whole thing, every ugly detail.

thirty-one

Thatcher rode into Buckman's Pride weary and downcast. His friend's pregnant wife was on a train, where he had paid an attendant to give her the best of care. He could only imagine what joy William would experience when his wife returned to him. Colleen mourned her actions of leaving her husband and rejoiced when Thatcher explained the changes William had made—how he longed for nothing more than to be reconciled and to be able to prove his love to Colleen. Thatcher knew there would be a happy reunion and prayed that all would go well with her trip. He prayed for William and the things he was facing at home with his father's illness.

If only Thatcher's own romance had turned out so well. Thatcher felt that he had ruined things between him and Meredith for good. It seemed that the harder he had tried, from the beginning, the more he had hurt her. He wasn't sure how it kept happening or why. But he knew he loved her, and he would hunt her down if it took every breath he had. He would never let her go until she understood how much he cared for her. But right now, he was only so tired.

He tied up his horse outside the Bloomfields' and knocked on the door. His friends received him warmly and showed him to a soft bed, where he slept the rest of the day and that night through.

At daylight, he started out for the logging camp.

The Bloomfields had told him that he had just missed Meredith. What a wonder he hadn't met her on the trail somewhere. He had arrived the same day Meredith had left. He didn't know her plans, what other logging camps she intended to visit along the way. He wanted to give her time to cool off before he showed up in New York City.

One thing he knew for sure. His logging days were over. He would give his resignation to the bull and pack up his belongings. He would stay the night and say farewell to his friends.

The bull took the news of Thatcher's resignation with little emotion. Thatcher headed for the bunkhouse. It was empty. He packed his things, then sat on his bed, wondering what his next move would be. He prayed, "Lord, you know the desires of my heart. Please, help me."

"Thatcher?" The words sounded soft, hesitant, familiar. But, it couldn't be. His head jerked around. It was! He jumped to his feet.

"Meredith. It is you." His voice held reverence.

Hers quivered in return, but picked up force. "I shall not let my vanity ruin my life. I came back for you, Thatcher."

He didn't know whether to laugh, cry, or throw himself into her arms.

"My sweet. I was going to come for you."

"We've wasted enough time, haven't we?" She took a hesitant step toward him. "Can you ever forgive me?"

He closed the distance between them and pulled her to himself, saying the words against her hair. "Forgive you? I love you. I always have."

She pushed back away from him, looked up into his dark eyes. "I want you to know everything. Please, let me explain."

He nodded and dropped his arms.

"I've been so proud and controlling with my life. I'm not happy with the way I've treated you and others. God has shown me a better way. I'm yours, if you'll have me."

"Have you? Meredith, don't you know? I was going to follow you and beg, plead for you to believe me and marry me."

She reached up and touched his face. "I believe you. I always shall from this day forward."

"Marry me?"

"Yes."

He stooped to kiss her, and Meredith thought that nothing

could ever be more beautiful than her life this day, with Christ's love, with Thatcher's. Her heart soared with emotion.

"Hmm-mmm." A deep clearing of the throat came from the bunkhouse doorway. They both looked up, and Meredith drew out of Thatcher's arms.

The man in the door said, "I don't believe we've been properly introduced. I'm Storm's brother."

Thatcher strode toward him. "I'm her fiancé."

Meredith smiled up at her brother. "Charles persuaded me to come back after you."

Thatcher looked at the man with surprise. "Then I know I'm going to like you a lot."

Charles chuckled. "We'll get along fine."

❧

The wedding was held the following Sunday in Buckman's Pride with all Meredith and Thatcher's friends attending. Both Jonah and Beatrice promised to bring their spouses to visit them. Jonah, Meredith was sure, would marry Amelia soon.

After the wedding celebration, Thatcher took Meredith for a stroll along the river.

"I really like Charles," Thatcher said.

"I'm so glad. I hope when he breaks the news that father takes it well."

"From what Charles says, he's trying to change. Are you anxious to see him?"

"Yes."

"We'll visit him on our honeymoon."

"I'm not expecting miracles, though."

"You should; we're living one."

"I know."

They stopped at a high bank that looked down over the water. The sun was just starting to set. Beautiful colors made a promising display, and hope for the future filled both their hearts.

"We'll camp our way to San Francisco and have our own private celebration there," Thatcher said.

"That could be expensive."

He pulled her close. "I can afford it."

She smiled up at him.

"Then we'll go to the land office and let you pick out the camps you want to visit."

"Any that I want?" she asked, even though they had already agreed upon all this earlier.

"Any. We'll find us a little cabin. I'll work and you'll write, undercover."

"And we'll stay as long as it takes to finish my story."

"Probably as long as you can stay cooped up in a small cabin is more like it." He bent and tasted her lips. They were sweet and gave promise of a wonderful life ahead for them. He drew back. "Let's go to the hotel, shall we?"

Meredith nodded shyly.

Thatcher took her hand, then began to chuckle.

"What's so funny?" she asked.

"I was just thinking of my father. When we move to Chicago, I'm going to love the moment he meets his new daughter-in-law. You're going to be such a sweet torment to him."

"I thought you wanted to make amends."

"Oh, I do. It's just when I think how you blew into my life, I can't wait to see what happens when you storm into his."

"I've been meaning to talk to you about that. Maybe we shouldn't use my middle name at first. I'd hate to give him the wrong impression."

Thatcher laughed again.

"Stop it," she said.

Heartsong Presents
Love Stories Are Rated G!

That's for godly, gratifying, and of course, great! If you love a thrilling love story, but don't appreciate the sordidness of some popular paperback romances, **Heartsong Presents** is for you. In fact, **Heartsong Presents** is the *only inspirational romance book club* featuring love stories where Christian faith is the primary ingredient in a marriage relationship.

Sign up today to receive your first set of four, never before published Christian romances. Send no money now; you will receive a bill with the first shipment. You may cancel at any time without obligation, and if you aren't completely satisfied with any selection, you may return the books for an immediate refund!

Imagine. . .four new romances every four weeks—two historical, two contemporary—with men and women like you who long to meet the one God has chosen as the love of their lives. . .all for the low price of $9.97 postpaid.

To join, simply complete the coupon below and mail to the address provided. **Heartsong Presents** romances are rated G for another reason: They'll arrive *Godspeed!*

A Letter To Our Readers

Dear Reader:

In order that we might better contribute to your reading enjoyment, we would appreciate your taking a few minutes to respond to the following questions. We welcome your comments and read each form and letter we receive. When completed, please return to the following:

Rebecca Germany, Fiction Editor
Heartsong Presents
PO Box 719
Uhrichsville, Ohio 44683

1. Did you enjoy reading *Storm?*
   ❏ Very much. I would like to see more books
      by this author!
   ❏ Moderately
      I would have enjoyed it more if _____

   _____

   _____

2. Are you a member of **Heartsong Presents**? Yes ❏ No ❏
   If no, where did you purchase this book?_____

   _____

3. How would you rate, on a scale from 1 (poor) to 5 (superior), the cover design?_____

4. On a scale from 1 (poor) to 10 (superior), please rate the following elements.

   _____ Heroine   _____ Plot

   _____ Hero   _____ Inspirational theme

   _____ Setting   _____ Secondary characters

5. These characters were special because_____

_____

_____

6. How has this book inspired your life?_____

_____

_____

7. What settings would you like to see covered in future
   Heartsong Presents books?_____

_____

_____

8. What are some inspirational themes you would like to see
   treated in future books?_____

_____

_____

9. Would you be interested in reading other **Heartsong
   Presents** titles?   Yes ❑   No ❑

10. Please check your age range:
    ❑ Under 18   ❑ 18-24   ❑ 25-34
    ❑ 35-45   ❑ 46-55   ❑ Over 55

11. How many hours per week do you read?_____

Name _____

Occupation _____

Address _____

City _____ State _____ Zip _____